EXCITEMENT, DANGER, ADVENTURE . . .

Here are more than a dozen stories from the wonderful world of horses, including tales of:

"Two-bits," the big, clean-limbed chestnut police horse that is on the trail of a hit-and-run driver and a gang of thieves. . . .

A bronco-busting boy who dreams of the big rodeo and proves himself in the face of danger. . . .

Ramey, who loses his filly to a bet in a horse race—then wins her back with his love. . . .

Mary, who would do just about anything to have a horse of her own. . . .

And many more heart-warming stories—from the open range, to the rodeo, to the city—that will thrill and delight everyone!

Horse Stories

Edited by
David Thomas

AN ARCHWAY PAPERBACK
Published by POCKET BOOKS • NEW YORK

Horse Stories was originally published under the title *Teen-Age Horse Stories.*

An Archway Paperback published by
POCKET BOOKS, a Simon & Schuster division of
GULF & WESTERN CORPORATION
1230 Avenue of the Americas, New York, N.Y. 10020

Published by arrangement with Lantern Press, Inc.

ISBN: 0-671-44201-5

First Pocket Books printing February, 1964

20 19 18 17 16 15 14 13 12

Printed in the U.S.A.

Acknowledgments

GRATEFUL acknowledgment is made to all the authors of the stories appearing in this volume, their literary agents and the editors of all the publications in which these stories first appeared for their helpful cooperation.

Contents

A bugler blew "Stables" out of tune.

Horse Stories

Big Bones Rides Alone

FRANK H. CHELEY

OURS was a hunting expedition in every sense of the word. We were after food for the home ranch; we were after the continually marauding Cheyennes with whom our score was never even; we were after a dozen head of cattle that drifted in with a range herd and, last but not least, we were after horses—any wild horses we could get a rope on for they were bringing a good price, but particularly were we after the much-sought Silver Streak, a magnificent grey and tan stallion probably descendant from the famous Arabian horses of the ancient Coronado expedition which had long ago traversed the Grand Mesa. Yes, we were hunting—and as is always the case with Western ranchmen, seeking adventure.

It was the fourth year of the great drought—no grass, no water except on the high mesas and every water hole in the country dry save Twin-Springs in Paradise Valley, a neat little natural box canyon that appeared to be an ancient cave with the roof dropped in and an open water gap at each end caused by the two deep springs.

There were five of us in the party, four men and Big Bones McLean who although only a youth in years was larger and more powerful than anyone in the settlement; a quiet, determined chap who said little but who did much and was a general favorite because of his almost uncanny ability to ride anything on four legs. Old Bud McLean, his father, was in charge of the party. Tippy Canoe and Curly Thomas were seasoned cow hands while I was just a dirt farmer from Indiana and out West looking the play over preparatory to a move to new location.

We headed straight for Paradise for numerous reasons: Stray cattle would work to water; game, if there was any left in the country, would stay close to the springs, and Silver Streak, with his band of mares and their colts, would certainly keep the valley at least as a base from which to drink when safe.

It was two days of hard trail riding up over the Devil's Back Bone and through miles of slate shale. The first day passed uneventfully. Two or three times we thought we sighted Cheyenne scouts and even took several pot shots but the valleys were full of purple haze and more than likely, our Indians were slinking coyotes or hungry timber wolves from the lodge pole forests beyond.

At the camp fire that first night, Big Bones, who was always full of ideas, made a proposal. Why not fence off both water gaps with heavy pole fences, building a broad pole gate in the north end, making a snug corral of Paradise Valley, then attempting to trap our cattle, a little game and perhaps the stallion. It would take several long days of heavy labor, but all we had was time and why not? We considered, and upon arrival, the plan looked feasible, so, after setting up a crude camp against the east rim rock and hobbling our own horses securely on top of a bit of tableland that rose out of the floor of the valley, we set to the arduous task of dragging in dry poles for our barricades or rather of shoving them off the cliff from the cap rock.

We were of course working under primitive conditions which called for the combined ingenuity of the whole party, for with no shovels, no wire and only two three-quarter length saddle axes and a few extra lariat ropes, we were put to it to build securely enough to hold what would undoubtedly sooner or later be a prancing stampede. Furthermore, we were on short rations. On the way in we had picked off a dozen fat sage hens and we had plenty of split dry peas. Tippy had brought down two sizeable black squirrels in the pinyon flats. That with our bacon and beans was the commissary.

Big Bones' huge size and strength proved a boon and because the very idea was his, he felt special interest in and concern for the success of the venture. At night the big boy was almost too tired to eat and his sun-tanned face looked haggard and drawn. I almost felt sorry for him.

"Better go easy, Big Bones," cautioned his father laconically. "If you should get down on us here we'd just have to leave you here to ride old Silver Streak home." He laughed loudly at the very idea and we all joined in. Big Bones laughed too. "Stranger things than that *have* happened, Pop, and I have rid just as wild horses as Old Silver, but don't worry, we'll have plenty of time to rest when these fences are up—and starve, too! What I need is a big eatin' of good fresh beef. This here ladies' grub of yourn doesn't stick to my middle. I need beef stew and dumplings three times a day on a job like this."

So the joking continued and the fences progressed. The south fence was finished and tested and passed inspection. We moved camp to the other end of the little valley and set to it, knowing a bit better how to go at the job. At the end of the fourth day we had converted the finest bit of an Alpine valley in the Snowy Range into a corral with abrupt rock walls twenty feet high down both sides and stout pole fences at both ends. The next question was, how could we make it work effectively?

Tippy and Curly, after an all-day search, brought in a yearling deer. We laid off, rested, ate and slept. It was just four in the morning of that fifth day, when we were all wakened by the far away pounding of hoofs. The first crimson streaks of dawn were just coming over the eastern sky when a cloud of dust, led by as magnificent a wild stallion as has ever been seen in the West, raced toward the little valley and straight for our wide open newly constructed gate. We all stood shivering and holding our breath. Without a second's pause, they dashed through the open gate, too surprised to stop and unable because of the very lay of the land and the pressure from behind to veer to either side. Silver Streak was literally swept into our trap.

Like a shot, Big Bones dashed for the gate and in three jiffs, the poles were in place and forty to fifty horses were captive. We built our fire, got the coffee pot on and were just setting to congratulate ourselves when a herd of twenty range cattle, headed by a big roan steer appeared as if by magic at the gate and seemed quite bewildered to find the water hole fenced off. Then they got a whiff of our camp fire, wheeled and were gone again like scurrying clouds before a wind storm.

"They'll be back again," said Pop. "Let's drop the poles and stand guard to keep the horses in." We took our places hidden in the rough rocks and waited, for the cattle were what we had primarily come for. The horses were a by-product, but there wasn't a one of the five of us but that would give his very neck to own that silver stallion whether we could ever break him or not.

It was exactly at this juncture that the unexpected happened. We were not the only ones *hunting,* for suddenly from the top of the west rim rock came three shots, aimed deliberately at us.

We jumped for cover like so many frightened gophers.

"Cheyennes," called Pop. "Good thing they wasn't on our side of the corral or Silver Streak would have belonged to some good-for-nothin' Chief, yes, sir. Them Injuns has been driving them cattle. Now we're in for trouble." We scurried for shelter into the piles of porous, wind-eaten sand stone and held a council of war. If their tactics were true to form, they would first try to scare us out. If that failed, they would next try to steal our mounts or stampede them, and failing in that, they would settle down to pick us off one at a time or starve us out. These were the principles of Cheyenne warfare. However, we had the water and a few days' food, so we looked for a second surprise attack from a different direction.

"And that reminds me," said Tippy Canoe. "If them cayuses of ours ever get off that bit of a tableland and join up with them wild mustangs, we might just as well start walking home. One of us has got to get to 'em and stay with 'em, for things are gettin' plenty interesting."

While we held council of war from rock to rock, to our joy, in dashed the cattle, from all appearances driven, for they were running lame with tongues hanging out—famished for water. They never paused at the strange pole fence and bolted straight through the narrow gate like a stampede in a full flight and headed straight for the water hole. Behind them rode a dozen Cheyennes who swerved into the timber at sight of the pole gate.

In ten jiffs, the whole corral was in a wild pandemonium of milling cattle and wild horses, while our own hobbled mounts gazed down from their elevated perch and whinnied excitedly. Big Bones again worked his way from rock to rock toward the gate and then with a wild dash he was at it and in two minutes the top two poles were slipped into place and he was lost again in the rocks. I expected to see him topple over filled with arrows, but evidently our Indians were busy with other plans.

"There are ten of the varmints," he called. "I can see them just back from the rim rock. They are all mounted and holding council. Looks like a general war party and nine chances to ten they were headed for the settlement when they caught up with these cattle. Of course they'd have to be lookin' for trouble while we're all away. Let's sit tight and wait. Better yet, let's find good cover together near the gate, but if they open up our fence at the south end, we lose. But if they do as I think they will, they will leave a couple of braves to devil us and the rest will go on to the ranches while we're all here in our self-concocted trap."

Until mid-afternoon they marauded up and down the rim rock watching for a pot shot, wasting their ammunition while we played a waiting game. It then began to dawn upon us that night was going to bring a lot of complications entirely unfavorable to us.

"Quick as it's dark," said Pop, "we scatter—one at the gate, one at the south fence and Tippy and

Curly can bring our own mounts down to water, saddle 'em and be ready for a dash."

"I got a better notion," said Big Bones thoughtfully. "We got to beat them Injuns to the ranches without losing either the cattle or horses if we can help it."

"Sounds swell," said Tippy who was always a bit contemptuous with Big Bones' suggestions. "But just how are you going to maneuver *that* miracle?"

"Easy enough," laughed Big Bones, all aquiver with excitement. "Easy enough—if you're all game. You came here lookin' for excitement to break the monotony of life, didn't ye? Well, here it is. We'll quietly drive the herds toward the gate in the night, just easy like so as not to frighten them. If we can separate Old Silver and drive him to the south end we can rope him and drop him and blind him and get a saddle and a hackamore onto him in the night and keep him flat on his side till crack of day, then I'll ride him out. Of course he'll squeal and fight and carry on something terrible, but them Indians will think the critters are fighting for water and be watching all night at the gate for our escape, cause they think they have us trapped. With the first streaks of dawn, you all will release Old Silver with *me* in the saddle and then stampede the horses and cattle out of the gate and we'll ride the stampede. Once on the open mesa, Silver will lead out, fighting for his freedom. The mares will follow and you all can bring up the rear and pick off the Cheyennes as best you can. And let's lead the whole frenzied mass toward Red Valley and home. It's a chance and I don't see no other, and there is Mother and Sis and the rest that's got to be thought of. What you say?"

"Why, boy, you're crazier than ten loons," said Curly. "No man alivin' could ride that stallion in stampede over those slate flats. You wouldn't last a quarter of a mile, and what would be left of you would be trampled to pulp by the rest of the herd. I'd rather be scalped alive right here than try any such crazy trick as that. Nobody but a kid like you would have even thought of it."

"Nobody's askin' *ye* to try it," said Big Bones. "But there's Sis and Mom, I tell ye, at the ranch and not a mother's son of a man to protect 'em. There's a heap more than ten of them varmints—there always is—and they aren't going to let us amble out of this valley and take our cattle peacefully home. No, Curly, they is but one way—a terrible sudden surprise. They know Old Silver's speed same as we do and strength, too, but they don't know Big Bones. At daybreak I'm ridin' that stallion home unless you birds are scared to help me get on the hackamore and the blind. If you'll do that, I'll do the rest."

"But I've sworn to be the first man to sit Old Silver myself," grumbled Tippy, crestfallen.

"So you have, have you," said Big Bones, "so you have. I'd let you try it, Tippy, but you can't hold him. You just haven't got the strength. No, I've got to do it myself. I'm not hankering a speck for any glory. I've rid wild horses before, but there is the women folks. We darsn't chance it. Tippy, you can have Silver for all of me when I'm through with him, but it's me that rides him to safety or death at crack of day."

"You're dead right," said old Pop McLean. "We got to do it, boys, just as the kid says, but let's do it thorough and careful as we know how. I wisht it was mornin' now. Tippy, you and Curly get our horses off the flat and water 'em and hide 'em next the rim as near the gate as possible where they can't see the stampede. Joe, you take the gate and shoot to kill. I'll go with the kid to look over the play. Mind, it's team work that will do the trick—a slip may mean five scalps for the Cheyennes. Do you understand?"

Those were long hours! Big Bones turned his mount over to me, took his saddle, carefully worked over his handmade horse-hair hackamore and placed them on the rocks opposite the spot selected to "drop" Silver. The cow hands looked to their lariats and made careful plans for the roping of Silver; forelegs first and when down to tie quickly the hind legs and apply the blind. These operations were not at all new to them; they had handled many a wild mustang in just exactly that fashion until it was well nigh a fine art with them.

All was set; every detail arranged. Big Bones went off by himself out under the star light and into the jet black shadows of the rim rock to think through every move of his great adventure. Once safely through the gate, he would give Silver his head. He felt certain the great stallion would make for the big mesa. They would make time there. He could feel himself gliding through the air like an arrow and feel the very earth tremble under the pound of the stampede. Suddenly a cool calm possessed him just as it always did at the big Rodeo before his turn to ride came. He felt a deep sense of satisfaction and an assurance that he would win. He crowded all thoughts of failure or mishap out of his mind. He fairly exulted in his mighty strength. He whistled softly his favorite tune, "Bury Me Not on the Lone Prairie." Then he chuckled to himself. He *was* going to win. He always did. He *had* to win for the sake of all of those who were depending upon him in this emergency—depending upon him and his courage.

He was very close to the big stallion and he spoke to him in soft spoken tones.

"Take me home, boy, safely through thick and thin, boy; over those treacherous shale flats; up, up slate creek—to the home ranch. Take me safely, Silver—and—and—I'll give you freedom." He said it without thinking. It was a new idea, but it appealed mightily to his sense of fair play. "It's a bargain, boy, isn't it? We'll save the settlement yet and perhaps some day Tippy, if he lives through the stampede, may ketch up with you again."

Gradually the black night paled. The stars faded as if one by one they had gone to sleep. There was the faintest tinge of purple and old rose on the Eastern horizon. The hour had come! In ten minutes Big Bones would be making the wildest ride in all his experience on the most superb horse he had ever seen.

Pop McLean slapped his big son on the back softly. "I'll be seein' ya at the home place, son."

"Yep, Pop," said Big Bones. "Take care of yourself, Pop. Wisht I could ride for both of us today."

The four shadows moved toward Old Silver who raised his head inquiringly. There was nowhere he could bolt but straight forward. They must count solely upon his own great weight in the slip knot to throw him. No combined force in the corral could possibly hold him unless he automatically went down.

There was a plunge. Curly's rope tightened—almost the instant Tippy's lariat sung. Both were true. With a mighty snort, Silver went headlong and almost before he was flat Old Pop McLean had the front legs secure and tied and was struggling with the vicious head. Just how or when the blind was secured and the hackamore gotten on nobody knew, but in less than ten seconds all save Pop were struggling with the saddle.

"Now for the stampede," cried Tippy. "Look out for an arrow, Curly. You'll make a handsome pin cushion."

The horses snorted and were off. The cattle joined as if by pre-arrangement. Pop had cut the front legs free. Silver struggled to them, shook the eye blind in wild desperation and terror. The Senior McLean's cow pony, trained by long years, stood at his heels ready.

"God bless you, boy," cried Pop, as he released the hind legs with a sudden yank. The cattle and horses were just at the gate and in full flight. Big

Bones looked quickly over his shoulder to see his father safely mounted, then he released the blind and the great stallion, seeing the whole herd in full flight, bolted. The race was on! He cleared the gate with his mares, whinnying like a beast caught in a fire. Through the herd he went as if they hadn't been there at all. Instantly he was out in the lead. It was pale daylight, that was all Big Bones knew and that he was riding the most powerful animal he had ever sat upon. He crouched low and wound the end of the hackamore several times about his wrist for safety. It was daylight now and off to both sides the boy was conscious of separate groups of racing horses. He knew full well they were Cheyennes. It would be a plain case of the survival of the fittest, but his heart sang, his mighty back and shoulder muscles quivered. Cold shivers played up and down his spine.

The going on the mesa was splendid. He dreaded the slate flats for footing would not be so good but he also knew the Cheyennes must either close in or drop behind. He wondered if the rest of the party was safe in the pounding stampede. It was not long till he heard shots and knew that his party and the Indians were engaging in battle.

"Remember, Silver," he said over and over, "this day you earn your freedom." The great stallion seemed to understand for on he tore like the wind, blowing now and then but on a long even stride that was simply marvelous. On they went for two hours until a slight gap began to develop between the racing stallion and the herds behind. The gap grew. Big Bones was now far out in the lead, an excellent target for Indian arrows but there were none. The Cheyennes were far behind or else had taken a short cut down the South Pass for the settlements.

Big Bones tried to swerve the great animal, first to right and then to left in order that he might get a rear view but all to no avail. On went the great horse like an unspent arrow, seemingly tireless, determined. They were climbing a long ascent now. Ahead lay the rim rock and the shale flats. At the bottom on the other side lay the cabins.

At the summit the great horse came suddenly to a stop very nearly unseating the weary rider. Wheeling he raised his great head, eyes of fire flashing, and scanned the back track. Miles behind was a cloud of dust. Lost in it was his band of mares, and possibly the rest of the party. Not an Indian was in sight. Silver shook his great head impatiently. Was not this a good place to rid himself forever of his captor? Big Bones knew the signs. Here on this isolated mesa he was to break the stallion or be broken himself and pass out to become coyote feed.

The horse plunged, bounded, sun fished, floundered, scattered dirt into a dust cloud and then as suddenly stopped perfectly still and whinnied as if to recognize without further ado the superb supremacy of the great human bulk on his back. Big Bones spoke to him kindly.

"Now we're friends, Silver," he said. "We're friends and we're off to save the settlement. Tomorrow you can seek out your mares and be free again. Do you hear me—free!"

With a plunge, Silver was over the crown into the slate flats and was off again toward the settlement.

At dusk the lone rider dashed into the home place, weary and exhausted but with an exalted feeling in his heart. They had beaten the Cheyennes in.

Excitedly the women and children gathered, before Big Bones could dismount.

"Yes, Indians," he said. "Food and drink, quick, and then into the big barn, all of you."

He was on the ground now and to his dismay the great horse stood patiently. Quickly he pulled loose the saddle and with a quick slash of his knife cut away the hackamore.

"You're free now, my beauty—go," he said, "before these green eyed cow punchers catch up with us." But Silver refused to move. "Of course," laughed the tottering rider, "you must have food and water, too. Of course, and I'll leave the gate open for you and thank you, Silver—thank you." He led the weary animal to the pole corral, fed and watered him and then hurried to prepare for the Cheyennes who never came.

Late the next afternoon Pop and his party and the remnant of the stampede came into camp. Silver whinnied at their approach and nosed his mares almost affectionately.

Tippy Canoe was wild with glee at seeing the

stallion in the corral. "Remember, he's mine," he shouted to Big Bones as his first words of greeting.

"Yes," drawled Big Bones, "he's yours, Tippy, that is if you can ride him. If not, he's Curly's —and if you both fail, he belongs to Pop and me."

"*You've* got a grand horse," laughed weary Pop McLean, "and you're a grand kid, my boy. Your pop is still proud of ye. Come on now, Cheyennes and we'll settle this argument once for all."

The Black Horse

JIM KJELGAARD

THE July sun was hot, and the mountain was high. Jed Hale brushed the perspiration from his forehead as he mounted over the top. The coil of rope about his middle started to chafe. Jed unwrapped it and threw it on the ground while he sat down to rest.

He chewed thoughtfully on a straw and gazed down on the range of low hills that stretched as far as he could see. The big, saucer-like hoofmarks of the horse led down, but there was no particular hurry. The horse was not travelling fast. A man on foot, if he had two good legs, could see him as many times a day as he chose. But the horse could not be caught. Jed had known that when he started.

After an hour Jed rose to his feet, and at the limping hobble that was his fastest pace, started down the hill on the trail of the horse. If he could bring him back—something that fifteen men, each mounted on a good saddle horse, had not been able to do—he would get five hundred dollars. Raglan would pay that much for the black horse.

Jed had seen the black horse scatter Raglan's men. After two days of constant chasing they had finally run him into the stout log corral that they had built. The corral had been strong enough to hold any ordinary animal, but the black horse had crashed through it as though it had been matchwood when they tried to put a rope on him. The man on the wiry saddle pony, who had roped the horse as he ran, had barely escaped with his life. The pony had been dragged along for fifty yards, and would have been killed if the saddle girth had not broken. The black horse had rid himself of the rope somehow. It had not been on him when Jed caught up with him.

Jed's crippled leg gave him trouble going downhill. He was glad when he passed the summits of the low hills and descended into the valley where it was level. From a stream in the valley, Jed drank and ate his fill of the ripe raspberries that hung over the stream. He had had no money to buy supplies to bring along. But he needn't starve. More than once he had lived off the country.

A mile down the valley he came upon the black horse. It stood with its head in the shade of a tree, swishing the flies away with its tail. Noiselessly, Jed sank behind a patch of brush, and for four hours lost himself in staring.

It was the biggest and most magnificent horse Jed had ever seen. He knew horses. Product of a wastrel mother and father, victim of paralysis in his childhood, he had spent all his life doing chores for Raglan and other stockmen in the hills. He had never earned more than ten dollars a month, but he had dreams and ambitions. If he could get only ten acres of land for himself, he would somehow or other procure a mare, and make a living raising horses. That, for Jed, would be all he wanted of happiness.

The hill men had said that nobody could capture this horse; nothing could tame it. Every man in the hills had tried. The black horse wasn't fast. Three riders besides Raglan's men had had their ropes on him, two had had their ropes broken and the third had cut his rather than risk having his saddle horse dragged to death. Jed looked at the manila rope that he had again looped about his waist and shook his head. It was the best and strongest rope to be had, but it would not hold the black horse. Still—Raglan offered five hundred dollars.

Dusk fell. The black horse moved lazily out of the shade of the tree and began cropping at the rich grass that grew along the creek. For another half hour Jed watched him. When Jed was near the horse, he was not Jed Hale, crippled chore boy and roustabout. In some mysterious way he borrowed from the horse's boundless vitality. When the horse grazed too close to him and there was danger of his being discovered, Jed slipped out of his hiding place and moved half a mile up the valley. There, under the side of a mossy log, he made his bed for the night.

With sunup he rolled from under the log. He

had slept well enough and he was not tired, but even the summer nights were chilly in the hills. As briskly as he could, he set off down the valley to where he had last seen the horse.

The black horse was browsing peacefully in the center of a patch of wild grass that grew along the creek. For all the world he might have been one of Raglan's Percherons grazing in his home pasture. But the black horse was bigger than any Percheron that Raglan owned. There was another difference too, a subtle one, not to be noticed by the casual eye. When grazing, the black horse raised his head at least once every minute to look about him. It was the mark of the wild thing that must be aware of danger; no tame horse did that.

For a quarter of an hour Jed studied him from the shelter of some aspen trees. Then, as slowly as he could, he walked into the little field where the horse grazed. As soon as he left the shelter of the trees the horse stopped grazing and looked at him steadily. Jed's pulse pounded; the vein in his temple throbbed. Men with years more experience than he had said the horse was bad—a natural killer.

Recklessly Jed walked on. He came to within fifty feet of the horse. It made a nervous little start and trotted a few steps. Jed paused to make soothing noises with his mouth. The rope he had been carrying he threw to the ground. Two yards farther on the horse stopped, and swung his head to look at the crippled man. Jed advanced another twenty feet.

The black horse swung about. There was no fear

in him, but neither was there any viciousness. His ears tipped forward, not back, and his eyes betrayed only a lively curiosity.

In low tones that scarcely carried across the few feet that separated them, Jed talked to the horse. Still talking, he walked forward. The black horse tossed his head in puzzled wonderment and made nervous little motions with his feet. Fifteen feet separated them, then ten feet. The horse shone like a mountain of muscle and strength. With a sudden, blasting snort he wheeled and thundered down the valley. Jed sank to the ground; perspiration covered his face. He had done what no other man in the hills had ever done, been unarmed in striking distance of the horse. But the horse was not a killer. If he were, Jed knew that he would not be alive now.

Jed took a fish line and hook from his pocket, and picked some worms from the bottom of an overturned stone. He cut a willow pole with his sheath knife and caught three trout from the stream. He built a fire and broiled the fish over the flames. He was on a fool's mission. He should be back among the stockmen earning the money that would provide him with food during the winter to come. Deliberately he ate the trout. Getting to his feet, he put out the fire and struck off in the direction taken by the horse.

For another six days he followed the black horse about the low hills. Jed rested when the horse rested and went on when the horse moved again. For the six days the horse stayed within a mile radius of the small meadow where Jed had tried to approach him. Then on the seventh day, moved by some unaccountable impulse within his massive head, the horse struck across the low hills and did not stop at any of his customary grazing grounds. Patiently Jed gathered up his coil of rope and followed.

The horse had been foaled in Raglan's back pasture, and somehow he had been overlooked when Raglan took his stock in for the winter. They were, Jed guessed, travelling in a great circle and within a month or six weeks they would come back to Raglan's pasture again. It was only at rare intervals that the horse appeared at the pasture. His visits were always unwelcome. Numberless times he had lured mares into the hills with him, and only with difficulty had they been recaptured.

All day he travelled without stopping. It marked the first day that Jed did not see the horse. He was a little fearful when he made his bed that night under a ledge of rocks a dozen miles from where they had started. For two hours he lay peering into the dark, unable to sleep. He did not own the horse and could not catch him, and by spending his time following him he was only making it certain that he would have to live all the next winter on boiled corn meal when he was lucky enough to get it.

Nevertheless, he had to chase the black horse. If he could not come up to him again and somehow contrive a way to capture him, then nothing else mattered either. Finally Jed slept.

He was up the next morning with the first streak of dawn and he did not bother with a cooked meal. Some low-hanging juneberries served him for breakfast. He ate a few and picked a great handful to eat as he walked. Only when he was again on the trail of the horse did he feel at ease.

At twilight he found the horse again. He was quietly grazing in the bottom of a low and rocky ravine. Jed lay on top of the ravine and watched him. He had never been in this country before and he did not like it. The valleys were not gently sloping as in the low hills he had just left. It was a place of rocks, of steep ravines, and oddly enough, of swamps. The creeks were low and muddy, a good country to stay out of.

With night Jed moved a quarter mile back from the lip of the ravine and built a fire. He supped on berries, but rabbit sign was plentiful. With his knife he cut a yard from the end of his rope and unbraided it. Within a hundred yards of his fire he set a dozen snares, and curled on the ground beside the fire to sleep.

He awoke in the middle of the night. The air was cool. A high wind soared across the rocky ledge upon which he slept. Thunder rolled in the sky. The night was made fearfully light by flashes of lightning. Jed picked up a fat pine knot that dripped sticky pitch and stirred the embers of his fire. He lighted the knot at the embers and with it blazing in his hands, he made the rounds of his snares. There were rabbits in two of them. Gathering them up along with the unsprung snares, Jed made his way along the rocky ledge by the light of the pine torch.

Halfway around it he came to the place he sought. Close to the wall of the cliff a huge flat rock lay across two small boulders. The natural cave thus formed was full of leaves blown in by the wind. Laying the pair of rabbits on top of the rock, Jed crawled in among the leaves and in a few seconds he was fast asleep.

The second time he awoke in a wet world. Torrential rain had fallen while he slept. The sluggish stream that he could see from his retreat flowed out of its banks. Every leaf on every tree dripped water. A light rain still fell. Jed shrugged, and turned to the back of the cave. He built a fire in the dry leaves and fed it with wood that he split with his knife so it would burn. When both the rabbits were cooked and eaten, he wound the rope about him and set out once more to look for the black horse.

The horse was not in the same ravine where Jed had seen him last night. Jed glanced at the steep wall of the ravine and at the swamp at its mouth. The horse could neither climb one nor cross the other. Jed walked along the edge of the ravine; descending into it when he did not have to would be hard work and unnecessary. At the head of the ravine, where it ran onto the summit of the hill, he found the horse's tracks. He followed them.

For five miles the horse had walked across the level top of the hill. Finally, between a cleft in its rocky side, he went down into another of the steep little ravines. There was a trail five feet wide where he had half-walked, half-slid down.

The rain had stopped, but a wind still blew. Jed stood at the top of the path where the horse had gone down and watched it critically. The walls of the ravine were forty feet high and steep. At the bottom it was scarcely twenty feet across.

Jed worked his way along the rim of the ravine towards its mouth. He would descend into it ahead of the horse, and chase him up the ravine to safe travel on top.

Where the ravine led into the main valley was another of the dismal swamps, a big one this time, fully a mile across, and it ran as far up and down the main valley as Jed was able to see. The black horse stood at the edge of the swamp pawing the soft ground anxiously with a front hoof. Jed watched as he galloped a few yards up the grassless floor of the ravine, then turned to test the swamp again.

For the first time since he had been following him, Jed saw that the black horse was worried. He peered anxiously about. Somewhere in the ravine was an enemy that he could not see. There were rattlesnakes and copperheads to be found in great numbers in just such places, but the black horse was snake-wise; he could avoid these. Occasionally, a wandering cougar was known to cross the hills and to take a colt or calf from the stockmen's herds. That must be it. A big cougar might possibly be able to fasten itself on the horse's back, and to kill it with fangs and raking claws.

Ten feet below him a little ledge jutted out from the side of the ravine. Jed doubled his rope around a tree and slid down. For several seconds after he gained the ledge, he lay gasping for breath.

At a blasting neigh of terror from the horse he crawled to the side of the ledge and looked over. Below him the black horse stood with his head thrown erect, his nostrils flaring, and his eyes reflecting the terror they felt. Jed yanked the rope down to him and looped it over a rock. The horse was in danger, he had to get to him. A cougar would run from a man, even such a man as himself.

For fifteen painful feet he struggled down the face of the ravine. His crippled leg sent spasms of pain shooting over his entire body. Grimly he held on. Five feet more he descended. Then his crippled leg proved unequal to the task his mind had given it. He lost his hold on the rope and landed in a heap at the bottom of the ravine.

He sat up to look about. Ten feet in front of him the black horse stood rigid, staring up the ravine.

Jed shook his head to clear it and took his knife from its sheath. There was no time now for anything save finding and coping with whatever nameless terror beset the horse. He rose to his feet by sheer will-power putting strength into his legs. When he walked up the ravine, he passed so close to the black horse that he might have reached out and touched him if he had wanted to. The horse merely sidestepped a few paces and followed him with questioning eyes.

The cougar would now either attack or slink away. Walking slowly, searching every ledge with his eyes and missing nothing, Jed advanced. He could not see anything. But there was a sinister thing here that could be neither seen nor heard, only sensed. The air was growing more gusty; pebbles rattled into the ravine. Jed glanced anxiously back over his shoulder. If somehow he had missed the enemy and it had got behind him to attack the horse—. But the black horse still stood; from all appearances he had not moved a muscle.

Suddenly the silence broke. The black horse screamed, a long and chilling blast of fear. There came the pound of his hooves as he fled back down the ravine. Jed heard him splashing into the swamp. Simultaneously there came a deep-throated rumble from up the ravine, as a huge boulder loosed its hold on the canyon's lip to thunder down the side. It gathered others as it rolled. There was a stacatto rattling as shale mingled with the avalanche.

Jed sheathed his knife. Within a minute everything was over. A pall of shale dust hung in the air, but that was wafted away by its own weight. The avalanche, then, was the enemy. Animal instinct had told the horse that the slide was coming. The ravine was blocked to a third of its depth by a wall of shale and rock. A man could get over the block, a horse never could. With a shrug, Jed turned back to the swamp and to the horse.

The horse was a raving-mad thing. Ten feet from the rocky floor of the ravine he struggled in the grip of swamp mud that was already up to his belly. His breath came in agonized gasps as he strove with all his mighty strength to free himself of the slimy hand of the swamp. Slowly, inexorably, he sank. As Jed watched, he flung himself four inches out of the mud, and fell back again to sink deeper than before.

Jed walked into the swamp. It sucked at his bare feet, and sighed because it could not grip them. If he stayed out of holes, and stepped on grass tussocks wherever he could, he would not sink.

The horse was fast in the grip of the mud when Jed reached its side. It could not move but still tossed its head wildly. A sublime elation gripped Jed when he first laid a hand on the horse's back. He had, he felt, at last known a full moment in his life.

"Easy, old boy," he crooned. "Take it easy."

The horse swung its head about and knocked him sprawling in the mud. Coolly Jed picked himself up to walk back to the mired animal. Kneeling by the horse's shoulder, he ran his hand slowly up its neck.

"Don't be worried, horse," he pleaded. "Don't fight so, old fellow. I'll get you out."

Wildly the black horse struggled. Slowly, carefully, making no move that might alarm, Jed scratched his neck and talked to him. Finally the black horse stopped his insane thrashing and held his head still. Calmly Jed walked to the front of him. Instantly the black horse closed his jaws on Jed's arm. Jed gritted his teeth as the horse squeezed, but his free hand played soothingly around the animal's ears.

The horse unclenched his jaws. He pressed his muzzle against Jed's mud-caked body and smelled him over. Jed grinned happily. The black horse and he were acquainted. Now he could go to work.

The frenzied flight of the black horse had carried him a dozen feet from the floor of the ravine, and left him facing into the swamp. Still keeping up his murmuring undertone, Jed studied the situation. He had no lifts or hoists and no way of getting any. It was useless for him to try to pit his own strength against the sucking mud. Likewise there was no way whatever to make the horse obey his commands, and first he would have to get him facing back towards the ravine.

With his knife Jed set to work by the horse's side. When the carpet of grass on top of the mud had been cut away he could dig faster with his hands, but as soon as he scooped out a handful of mud another handful seeped in to take its place. Jed took off his shirt and returned to the ravine, where he filled the shirt with loose shale from the rock slide. As soon as he scooped away a handful of mud he packed the remaining wall with shale. That held. The horse moved against the wall as soon as Jed made enough room for him to move, and Jed was much encouraged. Then darkness stopped the work. After eight hours of steady labor he had turned the horse around at least six inches.

In the last faint light of day Jed returned to the ravine and got the coil of rope. The night would be a bad time. He did not think the horse could sink any deeper, but if he became panicky again he might easily render useless all the work done. With his knife Jed hacked off a dozen slender saplings, and carried them back along with the coil of rope. The black horse turned his head to watch when Jed started back to where he was; almost it seemed that he was glad of company. Jed threw the saplings down beside the horse, they were to be his bed. The rope he passed about the horse's neck, and made a hackamore that fitted over his jaw. With his head resting on the horse's back, he lay down on the saplings. The end of the rope was in his hand. If the horse should start to sink he would hold his head up as long as he could.

All night long Jed talked to the mired horse, calling him endearing names, soothing him with quiet voice whenever he became restless. A full two hours he spent caressing the horse's head with his shale-torn hands. An hour before dawn he went again to the bottom of the ravine. Daylight was just breaking when he scrambled over the rock slide. He picked a great arm full of the wild grass that grew in patches on the other side of the slide and carried it to the horse. Half of it he threw down in front of him, but when the animal had eaten that he took the rest from Jed's hand.

Doggedly Jed set to work with his knife and hands. It was devastatingly slow work. Take out as much mud as he could, and pack the sides with shale. Before the sun set the black horse was again facing the ravine. Furiously he plunged to reach firm ground. Jed quieted him. The time to make the test had not yet come.

Jed slept again beside the horse. When morning came he once more scaled the slide to get him grass, then he resumed his digging. He worked from a different angle this time. It was scarcely ten feet to stony footing. A yard in front of the horse he set to work clearing the mud away. When he got down to the level of the horse's feet he filled the hole with rocks and shale, and packed the sides with shale alone. As the day wore on he gradually worked up to the horse's breast. Two hours before sunset all was ready.

In front of the black horse was a ramp of shale and rocks, a foot high, a yard long, and four feet wide. Jed took the rope, one end of which still formed the hackamore, and ran it into the ravine. He returned to the horse. With his knife and hands he scraped the mud away from one of the horse's mired front legs. As soon as the pressure eased, the horse brought his freed leg to rest on the ramp and he raised his entired body two inches from the mud.

Jed ran back to the ravine. Taking the rope in both hands he pulled gently but steadily. The horse fought the rope a minute before he yielded to it. With a prodigious effort he placed his other forefoot on the ramp and, arching his back, he sent all the elastic strength of his muscles into his mired rear quarters. Jed heaved madly on the rope. The horse cleared the ramp with both front legs; for the first time his belly was clear of the mud. Jed gritted his teeth and pulled, the horse's hind hooves slid on the ramp. He leaped, and threw himself a yard through the mud. His front feet found a wisp of hard footing; he pawed wildly. A second later the black horse scrambled to the stony floor of the ravine.

Jed fell back, and for a few seconds yielded to the fatigue that was upon him. He had slept little and eaten nothing for three days. Dimly he was aware of an immense black beast standing over him, pushing him with its muzzle and nibbling him with its lips.

The horse's mane fell about him. Jed grasped it and pulled himself erect. He could not rest yet. The black horse followed close behind him. He nickered anxiously when Jed climbed over the slide and pranced playfully when he came back, his arms laden with wild grass.

Half the grass Jed left on top of the slide, the rest he carried into the ravine with him. He took away the hackamore as the horse ate, and fashioned a breast strap in the end of the rope. With utter freedom he dodged under the horse's neck and arranged the crude harness. Then he climbed to the top of the slide for the rest of the grass.

Jed shook his head worriedly as he surveyed the slide; a good team might not move some of the boulders in it. But perhaps the black horse—. He banished fear from his mind as he hitched the free end of the rope about one of the boulders, and with the grass in his arms went to the horse's head.

He patted the horse as it pulled at the hay in his

arms. Slowly he backed away. The horse followed and the rope stretched taut. The black horse stopped, and swung his head as he edged nervously sideways. Jed gasped. If the horse fought the harness now he could never get it on him again, and he could never get him out of the ravine. Jed stepped close to the horse.

"This way, horse," he murmured. "Look this way. Come this way."

He stepped back again, the grass held out invitingly. The black horse trembled and took a step forward. Pebbles flew from beneath his hooves as he gave all his enormous strength to the task in hand. The tight rope almost hummed. The boulder moved an inch, six inches.

Then in a steady creeping that did not stop at all it came away from the slide.

A week later a great black horse appeared in the upper pasture where Tom Raglan was counting his colts. The horse stopped while the tiny, emaciated figure of a man slid from his back. Incredulously Raglan approached them. The horse stood fearlessly behind the wasted man.

"You got him, Jed," Raglan said.

Raglan was no waster of words, but words were not needed. He was unable to tear his eyes away from the horse's massive legs, his splendid head, his flawless body, all the qualities that had here combined to form the perfect living thing.

"I got him, Tom," Jed Hale said, "and I brought him back like I said I would."

Raglan coughed hesitantly. Above all else he was a horseman. There was no need for Jed to tell him of the chase, or how the horse had been captured. Jed's sunken eyes, his skeleton body, his tattered clothes, the fingers from which the nails had been torn, told that story for all who could read. There was a world of difference between himself, the successful stockman, and Jed, the crippled stable hand. But they were brothers by a common bond—the love of a good horse. Raglan coughed again. Jed had indeed brought the horse back, but by all the rules known, the black horse could belong to only one man, the man who had brought him back.

"Jed," Raglan said slowly, "I never went back on my word yet, and I'll stick by the bargain I made. But that horse is no good to me." Jed stood without speaking.

"He'd kill anybody except you that tried to monkey 'round him," Raglan continued. "I can't risk that. But I'll go a long way to get his blood in my stock. Now there's a house and barn in my north pasture. I'll give both of 'em to you along with fifty acres of ground, if you'll take that horse up there and let me turn my best mares in with him. I can pay you thirty dollars a month, and you can keep every seventh colt. Do you think you'd just as soon do that as to have the five hundred?"

Jed Hale gasped, and put a hand against the black horse's withers to steady himself. The black horse laid his muzzle against Jed's shoulder. Jed encircled it with an arm. The black horse, the horse that could do anything, was his now. It was a little too much to stand all at once. Suddenly Jed remembered that he was now a hard-boiled stock owner.

"Why yes," he said finally. "If that's the way you'd rather have it, Tom. Yes, I guess I'd just as soon."

Lucky Star

PAT ALLARD

WITH dirty brown toes Carlos glumly traced horseshoes in the dust. Then sitting down on an empty pail, he put his head in his hands and covered his ears so he couldn't hear Mr. Richards and those Americanos around the corner of the stable, talking about selling "Estrellita." Of course they referred to the gangling black colt as "Blue Wind," but to Carlos he would always be Estrellita —Little Star. Whenever he looked at the foal, the young Mexican dreamed of glittering stars swept across a cold, black sky.

Carlos decided to move. The stable area at Caliente was so big . . . why did those cheap Americanos have to stand and talk where he could hear them. Their voices were loud and harsh and they sounded as if they had no love in their hearts. That was wrong. Carlos could not explain why, but it was. People who own and train horses must have love. Carlos had it—he loved the sleek black foal more than anything else in the world . . . even more than going to town on fiesta days, or the new Sunday *zapatos* (shoes) the priest had given him.

Now the men were coming nearer. Though Carlos pretended not to be listening, he heard every word.

"But, Mr. Richards . . . we'll pay any price you ask. Just name it and we'll give you the cold cash, won't we, Jake?"

"Yeah, yeah—cold cash—just make your offer."

"But, gentlemen! I don't want to sell Blue Wind. He's the finest colt I've ever bred. Why, I'd be mad to let him go. Look at his breeding. He's by Sir Gregory out of Lady Ellen and that's as . . ."

Carlos knew all about Sir Gregory. He'd heard Señor Richards tell how time after time that swift black stallion had worn down all opposition in the stretch and raced across the finish, a winner!

"Now see here, Richards. Why not consider the financial side of the matter?"

"Sure, look at your stable. You're broke and here we're offering you cold cash . . ."

Carlos didn't know what cold cash was, but he suspected it had something to do with hardness and cruelty. He didn't even like the sound of the words.

"Gentlemen," Mr. Richards' tone grew firmer, "I don't wish to sell Blue Wind. He is the finest horse I own, and I'd starve rather than lose him. Will you go now? I have to get ready for the fiesta, and there isn't much time."

The fiesta! Carlos had almost forgotten! Tonight was the night of the grand drawing and everyone would be there. Tonight the hills around the little pueblo would echo the gaiety and color of fiesta days—music, dancing and the laughter of tall, young *muchachos;* there would be dark eyed señoritas selling lottery tickets, and great baskets of polished fruit piled high in the market. Carlos loved it all—the crowds, the color, the music, and the *peseta*s that he got for running errands for the foreigners. Oh, tonight would be an exciting one!

"Okay, okay, we'll leave, but remember—we want that colt and we'll have him yet!"

"Get away from this stable and stay away!" Carlos heard Mr. Richards call after the two men as they climbed into a shining red car and drove off.

Their laughter echoed back on the wind. It made Carlos feel queer inside—a little like the time he ate too many *enchiladas,* but it was more of a fearful, empty feeling.

"Carlos! Aqui."

He sprang from the pail and raced over to Mr. Richards.

"Did you hear those men, Carlos?"

"Si, señor. Those Americanos are bad men. You won't let them buy Estrel . . . I mean, Blue Wind, will you?"

"Don't worry. I won't. They're just trying to scare me."

"Oh, I am so happy. The colt is so young and he will be a good racer, just like his father, *no piensa usted* (don't you think)?"

"Better, perhaps. And Carlos . . . there is something that I want you to do."

"Si?"

"All of the other men are going to the fiesta, so I want you to stay here and take care of the horses for me."

"Si, señor," Carlos answered meekly, "I will."

"Good boy! I'm going now and I won't be back until late. You stay right here. Don't go away for a minute!"

"I will take good care of the horses."

As the owner strode away, Carlos went slowly back and sat on the pail. He wanted so much to go to the fiesta! Why, he'd even saved the *dinero* (money) he got for his birthday to buy a lottery ticket. Now he would miss all the fun!

The sun dropping behind the hills told him that it was time to feed the horses. He took care of the older ones first, and then went to Lady Ellen's stall. He opened the door. As the mare turned her head placidly toward him, Carlos decided anew that he would rather be a groom than anything else in the world. Why, he got to know the horses better than even Mr. Richards himself!

Carlos turned the hay over and made a fresh bed for the colt. Estrellita, romping out from behind his mother, lifted a cold black nose and buried it in his groom's hand. Carlos put an arm around the gangling body.

"Estrellita, those Americanos can't take you away Señor Richards won't let them, and I won't let them either."

The colt snuggled up to the Mexican boy, who whispered in his soft black ear: "Some day you'll be a champion, just like your father. And you'll win trophies and cups and I'll ride you. The form charts will read—Blue Wind, Carlos Gonzales up—but when we're racing down the back stretch I'll whisper 'Estrellita' in your ear, and you'll understand and start to pull away from the field. It will be so wonderful!"

Estrellita whimpered softly as Carlos peered behind the colt's ear.

"There it is," he murmured, "the little white star. It's so small that Señor Richards and the others don't even know it's there. If they did, they would call you Estrellita instead of Blue Wind—just like I do!"

When pushed away gently, the colt ran again to his mother's side. *"Buenas noches,"* Carlos called softly and closed the stall door.

Carlos decided he would sit in front of the stalls and watch the horses, although he would not have to watch very closely. After all, with everybody at the fiesta, the stable grounds were deserted. He could hear the music and see the bright lights of the town. Everyone was singing and laughing, and peons were dancing in the streets to the beating rhythm of castanets. Carlos couldn't see those things, but he knew what it would be like. The music drifted to him quite distinctly. It wasn't really very far away. Why, he could run over, if he cut across the fields, and be back in ten minutes. There could be no harm in that—then he would be able to see the lights and fun after all.

As he rose, Lady Ellen and her offspring moved in the near-by stall. He paused—perhaps he shouldn't leave them. But what harm could come to them in such a short time?

Carlos thrust a lean brown hand into the pocket of his overalls.

It wouldn't take long. Just ten minutes or so . . .

His fingers touched the *pesetas* in the bottom of the pocket. He might even win the lottery!

Returning, Carlos's bare feet slipped as he ran through the wet grass of the field. He would have to hurry. He'd been longer than he expected—almost half an hour. The cockfight had been so exciting and he had bought a lottery ticket. Of course, he thought glumly, it wasn't the winning one, but he had had enough money left to buy some *dulces* (candy) and he was bringing one to Estrellita.

He climbed over the fence and started down the shed row. Suddenly, out of the darkness, he heard men's voices. They were coming from the row of new stables—the ones that the Americanos had rented.

Carlos thought the voices seemed familiar—they sounded harsh and cruel, as if they had no . . . that was it! It *was* the Americanos. But what were they doing here at night, when everyone was at the fiesta. They were coming closer. Carlos crept behind a bale of hay and held very still—scarcely breathing.

"That'll serve the old bird right!"

"Yeah!"

Shuddering at their sinister chuckling, Carlos watched while they walked through a patch of moonlight.

"We were lucky to find a colt that looked just like Blue Wind—coal black with no markings."

Blue Wind! Carlos's heart jumped. They were talking about Estrellita! They said he had no markings.

"We can pull out in the morning and get across the border by noon—with the colt *and* the dough."

"Yeah," came the tall man's reply, "we sure pulled a fast one on Richards!"

Carlos heard a door slam and saw the car pull away. He sprang from his hiding place and sped to Lady Ellen's stall. As he went in, she stirred and the black colt by her side rolled over.

"Estrellita," he called softly, "*Aqui,* Estrellita!"

The colt didn't come to him, so Carlos pulled him out into the moonlight. He looked just like Estrellita, but Carlos had to be sure. Pulling the colt's ear forward he peered behind it. There was no white star! He bent closer for a more careful inspection. No . . . it just wasn't there!

Suddenly the foal jerked away and ran to the other corner of the stall.

Why, he didn't even act like Estrellita, Carlos thought. He didn't brush against his legs or put a cold black nose on his hand! The foal wasn't Estrellita—it was a different horse—one that looked just like Lady Ellen's son—except for the white star!

Carlos knew now what had happened. And he must do something—this very minute!

He opened the stall and led the colt out. He must hurry before Señor Richards came back. Oh, he never should have left the stable. That was when it had happened. The two men must have watched and waited until he'd run over to the fiesta. They thought they'd outwitted the señor, but they didn't know about the star!

Quickly Carlos took the colt down to the new stable. He was certainly lucky that all the men were in town. He hurried, pulling the little foal as fast as he could go. Finally, he came to the Americanos' stables. They were deserted, but Carlos looked around cautiously before opening the first stall. It was empty. He went on to the next one—a brown gelding lay asleep in the corner. Finally, in the fourth stall he heard a horse stirring.

Carlos ran to the door and pulled it open. There in the far corner stood Estrellita, frightened and cold. Carlos rushed to him and laid his brown cheek against the colt's trembling side.

"Don't worry, Estrellita. It will be all right, but we must hurry and get you back to Lady Ellen's stall. It's getting late."

Carlos pushed the strange black colt into the stall, and led Estrellita out. The colt ran beside him as they raced down between the stables to Richards' stalls. When Carlos opened the door Estrellita rushed to Lady Ellen's side.

Soon the music faded and the lights began to dim. The fiesta must be almost over, Carlos thought, as he brought fresh hay into the stall. He would sleep with Estrellita the rest of the night.

About half an hour later he heard Señor Richards come up, talking to a friend.

"Oh, no, Thompson, I wouldn't sell the colt, and the men finally went away. I was afraid they might try something funny, so I left my Mexican groom here in charge."

"Can you trust him?" Carlos heard the other man ask.

"Trust him? Of course! He's loyal as they make 'em. Why, look," he added, flashing on his light, "he's probably been right there ever since I left."

Carlos opened his eyes and winked at his charge—and he would have been willing to bet his new Sunday shoes that Estrellita winked back. Anyway, he vowed, from now on he would always be worthy of Señor Richards' good opinion.

Two-bits of Traffic C

IRVING CRUMP

BRONX PARKWAY reached away like a long wet ribbon through the night with a vista of jewel-like street lamps. At the intersection of 210th Street the white traffic post stood out adding alternately green and red reflections along the wet pavement. There was not much traffic. Occasionally the glaring eyes of a car loomed up at the far off turn, came down the wet pavement. Some of the cars skidded a little when they stopped at the traffic light. Others came to a stop with the tires squeegeeing the wet pavements with a rubbery squeak. But they all stopped for the light; that is all but one.

Two-bits, the fine, big clean-limbed, chestnut police horse, the mount of Patrolman James Jennings, almost anticipated the fact that the driver of the car coming north intended to try and run the light. Some strange sixth sense, highly developed in horses of his breeding and training, and often called horse sense, warned him that the man driving this car was not the best kind of citizen. For one thing he was running with his bright lights on and that was not allowed within the city limits. Bright lights always annoyed Two-bits. He had heard Patrolman Jimmy say a lot of things about men who drove with brilliant headlights shining, and he had stood by and seen Jimmy give some of them one of those little slips of paper from the note-book he carried.

This fellow was going to get a bawling out, if not one of those slips. Two-bits knew it the minute he caught sight of the car coming up the drive. He and Jimmy had been standing in the shadow of some Parkway shrubbery. Two-bits heard Jimmy grumble something, and felt him fumble under his wet slicker for his whistle as his knees signaled to move forward. Two-bits stepped out carefully on the wet and slippery pavement, planting his rubber-calked shoes solidly to guard against slipping. And as he moved forward, he expected to hear Jimmy's whistle chirp shrilly.

Patrolman Jimmy did not blow his whistle, however, for the green light on the traffic post clicked to a change and red eyes gleamed in the darkness warning the oncoming motorist to stop. But as Two-bits advanced and the car came on with undiminished speed, the horse saw that the driver did not intend to stop for the light. In fact, Two-bits' quick ear heard the engine accelerate a little as the driver made a desperate effort to run the intersection on the red light.

The whistle chirped out a succession of quick blasts. And as it shrilled, Two-bits, with the fearlessness of a trained police horse stepped forward into the glare of the oncoming headlights.

The driver of the big closed car saw the policeman and his horse and heard his warning whistle at the same time, and instinctively he stepped down on his brakes; stepped down hard in fact. There was a shrill screech of bands clamping home followed by a hiss of tires sliding in the wet, then suddenly another shrill, rubbery squeek and things happened.

The big car began to skid. The heavy rear end whipped around, straightened a little, twisted the other way, and the car slid sideways straight for Two-bits and Patrolman Jennings. Two-bits tried to leap sideways out of the path, but his rubber-calked shoes skidded in the wet, and he fell as the car struck him. There was a crash of glass, a shout of anger from Patrolman Jennings as he struggled to throw himself clear of the saddle, then a general mix-up in which the slicker-clad policeman went sailing through the air to come down heavily on the wet pavement, and Two-bits went to his knees as the big car knocked his feet out from under him and skidded past.

Patrolman Jennings landed on his shoulder with such force that his head snapped downward against the pavement with a terrific whack. But he was a fighter and he did not remain unconscious long. Indeed, a few seconds after he landed on the pavement he struggled to his knees and tried valiantly to get to his feet. But his head whirled and the landscape swam before his blurred vision. His hands and feet became entangled in his rubber coat, too, causing him to fall again, and as he rolled over on the pavement he heard the thunderous roar of the car's motor as the driver opened it up once more and sent it speeding on down the Parkway out of sight.

"One of those blasted hit and run drivers," muttered Patrolman Jennings as he staggered weakly to his feet and turned toward his horse. Two-bits was on his feet, too, trembling in every limb and staring with ears cocked in the direction of the vanishing car.

The horse had not been down for long. Fortunately, the skidding car had not hit him solidly. He was falling when the tail end whipped around and sideswiped his left shoulder. He had felt the burning sensation of some broken glass hitting him and opening up a cut on his withers, but he had not been stunned as Jimmy was and he was back on his feet while Jennings was still rolling around on the wet pavement.

But his heart was pounding and his breath was coming in gasps, for his horse intelligence told him that he and his master had had a close call. With a snort he moved toward the policeman and nuzzled him affectionately.

"Reckless fools. They got away, too, and I didn't get a look at their license plates. Lights were too bright. They blinded me. Didn't even see what kind of a car it was. It looked like a Cadillac, but I couldn't be sure. Two-bits, I wish you had sense enough to get their number. We might stand a chance of finding that car again if you had."

But Two-bits, with his horse instinct had marked that car more accurately than Jimmy could have marked it if he had seen the license plates. What did a set of numbers amount to anyway? They could be changed too easily. Two-bits had other and better methods. His keen sense of hearing had indelibly registered the sound of the motor: marked it as a fearsome sound different from the sound of any other car, as the noises of motors differ from each other. His keen eyes, too, had registered the form, size and color of the car as it fled off into the night and he would never forget it. Two-bits, like all horses, never forgot anything that caused him an injury.

And that car had injured him. It had not broken any bones fortunately, but it had bruised and skinned his side and glass had opened a wound in his shoulder. Patrolman Jennings found the wound as he passed his hands gently over the horse's mud-smeared and quivering flanks.

"They did hurt you, didn't they, old fellow? Looks like we would have to have a few days off, you and I, to get over being banged up this way. I got jiggered up a little myself." He led Two-bits to the side of the road. Then he went back to where a lot of broken glass gleamed in the lamplight.

"Busted a window, and a headlight, too, and—what's this?" Jennings bent over a wet object in the road and picked it up. It was a bolt of silk wrapped in wet paper that showed a brand mark.

"Silk. Standard Mills, too. Jingo! No wonder those birds didn't want to stop! A bunch of silk thieves—part of Lefty Colter's gang that has been robbing the Markison silk warehouses, I'll bet a hat. That's the second time I've had a brush with that gang and they've got away clean again. That car was full of silk, and this piece fell out when the window busted, that's what happened. I owe those birds something and I sure wish I could have nailed them that time."

With the bolt of silk in his hand Patrolman Jennings stood in the road staring in the direction the departed car had taken. But as he stood there, once more the lights began to swim in his blurred vision. He turned toward Two-bits and tried to reach him. But even as he took a forward step his legs doubled under him and he crumpled in the road, only partly aware of the fact that Two-bits had come to his side and now stood over him protectingly as he nuzzled him affectionately with his cold, wet muzzle. Only dimly did he realize, ages later it seemed, that a brother officer found him and took charge of his horse while an ambulance carried him to the hospital.

Jimmy Jennings and Two-bits had come into the

New York Police Department about the same time. Two-bits had come into the Department after a course of rigorous training at the stock farm where police horses are reared and trained for service. Jimmy Jennings had become a member of the Department by way of the Civil Service examinations and two months in the school for policemen.

Jennings was a westerner from Idaho, stranded in New York when a rodeo company in which he was doing some exhibition riding met financial disaster. Jimmy, just past twenty-one, had only a silver-mounted prize saddle and a few dollars to his name. The saddle brought him eighty dollars, capital on which to live while he started job hunting. The only job in the whole city that interested him was with the mounted squad of the Police Department. He found that there was soon to be examination for new policemen. He made application, took the examination, and because of his high school education, he had little difficulty in passing. Also because of his excellent physical condition and the fact that he was such a superior horseman there was no doubt in the minds of the officials where he would best fit into the department. He was immediately assigned to the mounted section of the traffic division and Two-bits was his working companion.

"By Jingo, you're a horse," said Jimmy enthusiastically when he saw Two-bits for the first time in the department's stables. "You're a horse with a heap of intelligence. I reckon you and I are going to be good pals."

As for Two-bits, when Jimmy Jennings, in his blue uniform, came into his stall, and ran a soothing hand over his flanks, and scratched him under his jaw, where all horses like to be scratched, he took one sniff, then rubbed his nose affectionately against Jimmy's shoulder, as if to say:

"By Jingo, you're a man. You're the kind who knows horses and loves them. I'm going to be proud to work for you and we sure are going to be good buddies."

And they were. For a year now they had been working together on the Parkway, where all young horses and young cops of the mounted department are stationed first. Together they had experienced the hardships and unpleasant weather that go with the life of a policeman. They had had some thrills and made some arrests together and once they had heard bullets whistle their deadly chorus close to them. That was with their first close shave with the Colter gang of silk thieves. They had got a broadcast to watch for a certain stolen car with bogus license plates, and one afternoon the very car they were watching for turned into the Parkway at Harrison Street right under their noses.

Patrolman Jimmy spotted the vehicle and blew his whistle for it to stop. But it did not stop. Instead it swung around the corner and into the Parkway at full tilt. Patrolman Jimmy and Two-bits tried to get in front of the machine. But they did not move fast enough. As it sped past them, Jimmy yanked his Police Special and fired a shot over the top of the car to warn the driver. But the short, dark-faced, ratty-eyed man did not stop. Instead he stepped on the gas, and at the same time three men in the car opened up at Jimmy and Two-bits with automatics, through the car window. Those bullets hummed close, but Two-bits was not afraid of gun fire. He had been pretty well schooled in that sort of work at the stock farm where he was trained. Nor did the bullets disturb Jimmy. The only thing that annoyed him was the fact that, after blazing six shots at the car and perforating the back of it thoroughly, it got away from him.

He had managed to cripple it up pretty well, however. One of his slugs went through the gas tank, and the machine was later found on the outskirts of New Rochelle, out of gas. It had been abandoned and left at the curb, and it was found to be loaded with silk, stolen from the Markison silk warehouses.

And here, evidently, was a second car used by the same gang that had got away from Jimmy, for there was no doubt in his mind and in the minds of his superiors that some of the members of the Colter gang had been in the automobile that had skidded into him and Two-bits.

They were a happy pair when they were together again and back on patrol duty. Some shifts had been made. Younger policemen had come into the mounted department and were placed on patrol up on the Parkway, and Jimmy, with Two-bits, was transfered to Traffic C, down in the vicinity of

Thirty-fourth Street and Fifth Avenue. Jimmy protested at first. He explained to Captain Mulcare that he wanted to continue on the Parkway Patrol and catch some of those Colter thieves.

But Captain Mulcare told him that some of their best detectives had been put on the Colter silk job, and that he was a traffic cop and not a sleuth. Anyway he was going down in the busy silk district where the Colter gang operated, so he might run up against them again.

They had miles of city streets to patrol, moving from one traffic post to another, relieving officers on duty for brief intervals during the day, and at night, when they were on the late shift, traveling block after block east and west of Fifth Avenue watching for trouble on the side streets, or keeping the late traffic moving on the main thoroughfares.

Patrolman Jimmy, in a measure, forgot about the accident and the car that had caused it, with his new duties. But Two-bits did not, and had he been able to communicate more plainly with Patrolman Jimmy he would have told him some things that would have startled him and made him marvel at his own stupidity. For instance, he would have told him that once during the six o'clock rush of traffic up Fifth Avenue that car passed so close to them that he, if he had not been afraid of it, could have touched it with his nose. Patrolman Jimmy, directing traffic, felt Two-bits shy and heard him snort. He saw his ear cock as he stared up

Fifth Avenue, but Jimmy ignorantly blamed the animal's restlessness on the fact that they were just taking in a big flag that hung out of the windows of one of the hotels, and he laughed at Two-bits.

But that was not the last time the car passed them. On two other occasions it was part of the steady stream of traffic that flowed up Fifth Avenue while Two-bits and Jimmy were on patrol, and once it actually stalled within thirty feet of them, in a traffic jam. Two-bits did a lot of backing and filling then and considerable snorting and pawing trying to tell Jimmy that the car was there, and that the man at the driver's wheel, the one with the pasty yellow complexion and the mean eyes, was the fellow who always drove it. But one car in a jam of traffic did not mean anything to Jimmy, and anyway he was too busy trying to help two brother officers unsnarl a tangle at Thirty-ninth Street before the lights changed and made things worse.

Two-bits could not understand why, when he told him so plainly on more than one occasion that the car that had injured them both was within his grasp, Jimmy did not stop it and give the driver one of those white slips. Yet Jimmy Jennings did many things that were beyond Two-bits' understanding, so the horse let it go at that and continued to keep a watchful eye and equally attentive ear on the alert for the car that had run them down.

It was an evening when they were on the shift from twelve o'clock in the afternoon to twelve o'clock at night. Two-bits directed traffic for Jimmy for twenty minutes while Jimmy gossiped with Pat McCarthy. Then they started east toward Herald Square where they looked things over. They crossed Sixth Avenue and moved east along the now quiet and deserted block in Thirty-fifth Street. There was a car parked well up the block in front of one of the several dingy old, and, apparently, unoccupied brownstone houses toward Fifth Avenue. It was out of the glow of the street lamp and Two-bits could not make it out very well, though he had a premonition that he knew the vehicle, and he cocked his ears at it and sniffed hard as he moved forward.

Jimmy saw those cocked ears and remarked about them.

"Only some old night-hawker of a taxi cab, Two-bits. What you so suspicious about? Driver's probably gone to get a bite to eat. It's funny, though, why he should leave it in the middle of the block that—sa-a-ay you, what's the matter, Two-bits? You're jumpy.

"By George. Been in a smash sometime ago. Left side was hit. Lamp busted. It's a Cadillac, too, and . . ." Jimmy rode closer and bent out of the saddle. "Front door handle has been knocked off. That's a new one on there now, and . . . sa-a-ay, it couldn't be this is the car that hit us? And you sort of recognize it, don't you, Two-bits? I wonder now . . ."

Jimmy glanced up and down the deserted street, then back at the house again. But he did not look back quickly enough to see a face vanish from one of the darkened windows of the second floor, although Two-bits saw it and snorted anxiously. It was the pasty face of the man who always drove the car.

"I should investigate that place I reckon. But if I try it alone, whoever is in there will get away from me," cogitated Jennings. "It's too easy for them to slip out the back way while I'm getting in the front, or pile out the front way while I'm muscling my way in through the rear. I'd better get help. Come on, Two-bits."

Jimmy swing the horse around. There was a police signal light and call box at the end of the block on the Fifth Avenue corner.

But even as his fingers shoved in the little brass stub that set the green light flashing, Two-bits snorted and threw up his head as he cocked his ears forward. At the same time Jimmy heard the rumble of a motor starting to life down the block.

"They saw me snooping and they're trying to make a getaway. Come on, Two-bits. We've got to stop 'em and look 'em over."

The motor was under way already. In low gear it was drawing away from the curb. Jimmy realized that if they were going to overtake the machine they would have to catch it before it shifted into high. Fast as Two-bits was, the animal could never hope to overtake the car once it really got going.

Two-bits put every ounce of strength and speed into his dash down the block.

Faster and faster traveled Two-bits, cutting down the lead of the car. But faster and faster traveled the car, too. When Two-bits was twenty feet behind the machine it was rolling along in second speed, almost as fast as Two-bits was galloping. Ugly faces were peering out of the window. Two-bits thought he saw the gleam of a revolver. So did Jimmy. He yanked out his own then, and leaning low along Two-bits' neck, he spoke to him.

"Faster, feller! Faster! We've got to get that outfit this time. We'll look like a pair of palookas if we let 'em get away from us again."

Two-bits seemed to realize that they would be disgraced if they let that car lose them and with a valiant effort he redoubled his speed. In three or four terrific jumps he was almost beside the car as it sped toward Sixth Avenue. But the driver was stepping down harder on the gas as he strove to accelerate the engine and shift into high. The motor coughed and sputtered for a moment, and bucked a little with the way the gasoline was flooding the carburetor. Then suddenly came a wrenching, grating sound and the clash of gears as the driver threw the machine into high and shot it forward.

Jimmy Jennings, in the saddle and within a few feet of the machine, knew that there was but a split second left to him and Two-bits to apprehend the fugitives. There was only one thing for Jimmy Jennings to do, and he did it.

Leaning forward in his saddle he hooked the fingers of his left hand under the upper edge of the open window beside the driver, at the same time he allowed the momentum of the car to drag him clear of his saddle. It was a simple trick. He had done it many a time bull dogging steers or changing horses at a fast canter out West. But a lot depended upon it this time. From the saddle he must swing down onto the running board of the car and hold fast in spite of the high speed the car was traveling. If he missed that running board and failed to swing aboard that racing car he might fall and be dragged under the wheels.

But Patrolman Jimmy did not miss the running board. As he shot clear of the saddle, he pulled himself toward the car and timed his feet to drop nicely. They landed perfectly on the running board with a heavy thump and the next instant Jimmy was standing beside the driver fiercely clinging fast with one hand and shoving the hard barrel of his service revolver into the man's back with the other.

"Stop that car and do it quick, if you don't want to be stopped yourself," snapped Jimmy crisply.

But the man stopped for another reason than the revolver prodding him between the ribs. The car had reached the corner of Sixth Avenue, at that instant, and without warning a trolley car rumbled to the crossing and stopped, blocking the way. The driver of the motor car saw that a fatal crash was imminent unless he applied the brakes forcefully, and he stepped down on them hard. And while Patrolman Jimmy was grimly trying to keep from being flung from the running board, a policeman leaped from the trolley car while another one sped across Sixth Avenue, and a third, none other than Sergeant Peacock, Jimmy's immediate superior, came running up from Thirty-fourth Street, all summoned by the flashing police light and the shrill of Jimmy's whistle.

"What's all this? What's the trouble, Jennings?" demanded the Sergeant as Jimmy dropped from the running board still keeping the driver covered with his revolver. Then as he peered into the car window he exclaimed:

"Why, by jove, you've arrested Lefty Colter and four of his gang! Good work!"

"I don't know who my prisoners are but this is the car that ran me and Two-bits down on Bronx Parkway a couple of months ago. And if one of those birds is Lefty Colter, I've found the gang's hangout all right. It's in a brownstone house, up the block there," exclaimed Patrolman Jimmy.

"It's the hangout of the Colter gang, I'm sure. We've got the silk robbers, fellows, and got them cold. Jennings, this is a mighty fine piece of work and you'll get a lot of credit for it, let me tell you. There have been a dozen department detectives on the trail of these fellows."

"Well," said Patrolman Jimmy with a smile, "my little ol' horse, Two-bits, he deserves most of the credit. If it hadn't been for him, I never would have identified that Cadillac car nor stumbled onto this place either. Look at him. Sergeant, he's a horse and I don't mean perhaps. He gets an extra quart of oats for this when we get back to the stables tonight if I have to buy 'em myself."

Jingle Wears His Spurs

DAN SELLARD

THROUGH the cracks in the old box stall under the grandstand of the Molalla Buckeroo Grounds, the roar of the Independence Day crowd filtered in and fell unheeded on the ears of "Jingle" Laraday. Savagely he tugged on the cinches of the saddle astride the clean-limbed bay that his father used as a roping horse. Even a firecracker exploding violently on the roof of the old box failed to jar him from his thoughts.

For Jingle was sore. Rather, he was given to righteous indignation. All season Bill Laraday had allowed his son to understand that when they came to Oregon, Jingle could enter the bronco busting contest in the rodeos. But now that they were actually on the spot, old Bill refused to let the boy ride—stating calmly that he was too young to enter anything but the free-for-all race.

Thinking of this, Jingle clinched and unclinched his grip on the saddle until his hands ached. So absorbed did he become in his dark thoughts, he failed to notice a pair of keen, gray eyes peering at him around the corner of the doorway. The owner of the eyes, a grizzled, feather-bedecked Indian, stood sagely watching the boy for a moment.

"What grim thoughts," he asked, "trouble our most expert rider?"

Jingle glared at his discoverer. "Expert rider, am I? Then why can't I enter the events that count? All I ever do is ride in the races, and that's no fun."

The old Indian, whom Jingle knew and respected as Two Crows, chief and eldest member of the Molalla tribe, smiled at the irate lad.

"Small deeds," he replied, "often count big, and those that seem big aren't always so. Our young bucks need not risk necks to gain favor in the eyes of others. Little things count big, too."

He turned and walked off.

Eyeing the leather-backed form, Jingle wondered just what he meant. Bill Laraday said the old Indians were the smartest men in the country. Maybe the chief knew what he was talking about. Maybe, if you waited a while, your chance did come; but gee! it certainly was hard waiting.

The saddling done, Jingle started to polish the bits of silver on the horn and skirts of the saddle. Attached to the skirt was a large silver plate which read: "To the champion all-round cowboy at Cheyenne, 1938." Jingle ran his fingers over the letters lovingly. After all, they didn't come much better than his dad—even if he couldn't understand how his son felt.

Casting his eyes about for a glimpse of his father, Jingle almost ran into a group of people entering the grounds. They were gawking about in a way which indicated that a rodeo was all new to them. Seeing the boy dressed in the rough clothing of the range, they instantly gathered round him and plied him with questions.

At first, Jingle tried hard to ignore them the way the other punchers did, but finally he answered, with something of a swagger: Yes, he rode in the races; and no, he didn't think it was so dangerous if you were lucky and watched your step. Then, spying his father, he excused himself and walked away on his high heels. Doggone tenderfeet! They were always bothering a man just when he was busy. Inwardly, however, he swelled with pride at being such a point of interest.

Bill Laraday, a tall, sun-tanned rider in a huge pearl-gray sombrero and lambskin vest and chaps, called: "Got Shotgun all ready, Jingle?"

"She's all ready but the bridle, Dad."

Running to the trailer, Jingle got out the bridle. He slipped it over the mare's head, and she took the bit easily between her teeth. Then he led the horse briskly to where his father was buckling on his spurs.

As Laraday, senior, took the reins and swung expertly onto the mare, Jingle asked the question which had been uppermost in his mind all morning. "If I win the race this afternoon, will you let me enter the bucking contest tomorrow?"

Bill sighed, "I'm getting tired of your asking me that over and over again. When the time comes, you'll get to ride; and until then don't bother me with silly questions."

He galloped off. Jingle turned and kicked a post of the corral viciously. It was always the same old story. He couldn't even get to first base with his father. Well, he'd show him! He didn't know how, but he would.

The next moment the public address system started announcing the grand entry parade. Some real action would come soon. Now the announcer was introducing the officials, the dignitaries, and the outstanding riders. Boy, he'd give anything to be out there and be introduced as the "World's Champ Bronc Buster." Jingle could just see himself on a peppery horse with silver trappings, prancing about in front of the cheering thousands.

Hearing a commotion toward the bucking chutes, Jingle sauntered over to discover what it was all about. Now he could see—it was that ornery old critter they called "Dutch Oven," meanest bucking horse in the business, known from coast to coast among Rodeo circles as bad luck, and feared by the best of the busters. He was battling the cowboys who were attempting to force him into the chute where he would be saddled and mounted. As yet, no one had stayed on him the required ten seconds, and he had even trampled three riders to death. Jingle gripped the top rail of the corral tensely, thinking: "I bet I could ride him down. If they'd only give me a chance!"

Turning from the corral, Jingle walked to a point where he could watch the riders being presented to the crowd. He saw old Two Crows standing in front of the grandstand; and as he watched him, the old chief's words of wisdom came back to his mind. Maybe his chance would come today!

"First event on your program this afternoon is the bronc riding from chutes," the announcer blared. "Keep your eyes on chute Number Four at the north end of the arena. The 'Texas Kid' is coming out on Dutch Oven, as ornery a critter as ever bucked, and never ridden the necessary ten seconds."

Evidently Tex was having trouble boarding the cayuse, for there was a continual banging at the gate of the chute. The black hat of the rider could be seen bobbing madly about, and the man at the gate stood tensely waiting for the signal. Suddenly the gate swung open. The coal-black stallion twisted out into the arena. With heaving flanks and rolling eyes he gathered his muscles and lunged straight into the air, nearly falling over on the clinging rider. But Tex yanked on the reins, and the brute hit the ground joltingly on all fours.

"He's going over on Tex," thought Jingle.

Standing with braced feet, tight muscles and bated breath, Jingle could feel every jump of the wild horse as if he were in the saddle instead of Tex. Hunching his shoulders, he clamped his teeth together as the animal again surged into the air.

Apparently he had read the horse's intentions correctly, for on the next jump Dutch Oven fell completely over backwards. Tex, however, expertly twisted from the saddle and jumped clear of the huge shape hurtling to the ground. But in doing so he had lost the stirrups, thereby disqualifying himself. To the crowd, though, it was a matter of life or death; and Tex got a big hand as he walked away disgustedly, picking up his hat near the chutes. Jingle expelled a long breath from his tortured lungs. He'd give his eyeteeth to have been out there!

Since it was nearly time for his race, Jingle waited no longer. He ran to the trailer which served as his home, and hurriedly changed from overalls to a pair of tailored riding pants and a scarlet shirt. He combed his hair and adjusted his neckerchief with a holder made of steer horn. After pulling on his boots and wiping them off on a spare saddle blanket, he proudly produced a pair of shining silver spurs from a buckskin bag.

As he adjusted them on his high-heeled boots, the flashily dressed young rider smiled because their jingling was responsible for his nickname. He took special pride in these engraved Spanish spurs for they had been given to him by an old pal of his father's, Will Rogers, when Will was riding the circuit with the rest of the boys. Jingle thought wistfully, "I bet if Will was here now, he'd get them to let me ride in the big events."

He cut his reflections short, because the noise of the crowd told him that the bull dogging event was going strong, and he had yet to saddle his mount.

With a merry tune from the rowels on his spurs he strutted down the rows of stalls to one marked "J. Laraday." His turn of the button on the half-door was answered by a nicker from within; and as he entered the box, he was met and nearly pushed out again by a beautifully spotted gelding—none other than "Comanche Paint," pride and joy of the Laraday ranch. The length of the slender legs and the barrel-shaped chest told an expert eye that this was the type of horse bred in Kentucky and raised to work stock on the broad plains of Texas. Not sturdy enough for roping calves or bulldogging steers, the Paint was invaluable for running the short distance races of the rodeos or the small racing meets of the West.

Jingle reached into the pocket of his trousers and brought forth two white cubes of sugar. Comanche Paint clamped his teeth eagerly on his expected delicacy and crunched until every particle was devoured. Jingle patted the long neck and led the horse out to the trailer. He slung a bright-colored blanket on the glistening back. Next came the single-rigged saddle, and he tightened up the leather cinches firmly. After buckling on the headstall and bit, he mounted and trotted briskly up and down between the rows of trailers and stalls until the horse panted a little and a fine sweat broke out on his shoulders.

Soon the broadcasting system called "boots and saddles" for the fourth event, and Jingle trotted Comanche Paint into the arena.

When he thought of it later, the race that afternoon seemed almost like a dream. Things happened so swiftly that what had actually taken nearly half an hour seemed only a few minutes. His only real competition had come from Jimmy Daily, son of the Texas Kid, with his Morgan-bred mare. Jingle, however, knew how to take care of that; and he had won by his wild dashes around the turns, figuring that Daily's heavy mare couldn't take them as fast as Comanche Paint.

The next thing that seemed real to him was meeting his father at the gate. As his parent started to congratulate him, Jingle said, "Heck, it isn't anything to win these two-bit races. I could be winning the bucking and other big-money events if I was allowed."

Shaking his head sadly, Old Bill answered slowly: "If you don't stop hinting and asking about that all the time, I'm going to make you quit riding even the races. You win something, and you think you're the best puncher in the game. I don't know what's got into you lately."

Before Jingle could hatch up a retort, water welled in his eyes, and a lump rose in his throat. To hide his emotions, he walked his horse toward the stalls.

In a few minutes, the shaking of the bleachers above the feed room told him the afternoon's show was over. As the chattering throngs filed by, he watered and fed both of the horses and stalked over to the trailer. Already cleaned up, Bill awaited him as if nothing had happened.

"Want to go grab something to eat, Son?" he asked.

For a moment Jingle glared sullenly at his father, then turned and walked off, thinking: "Maybe if I refuse to talk to him for a few days, he'll feel sorry." Behind him, Bill merely stood watching his son before strolling away in the opposite direction.

When his father had left, Jingle circled back. He figured he'd wait until the riders had a chance to eat; then he'd go down to headquarters and talk to the Texas Kid and the rest of the boys. Leaning against the streamlined trailer which accompanied him and his father wherever they roamed, he could hear the clamor of the near-by carnival and smell the food frying in the hamburger stands. Now and then a shout broke through the dull roar, and here and there he could see a bright light flashing though it was not really dusk yet. He knew both sides of the town's main street were lined with hundreds of canvas-topped concessions that followed the rodeo business just as they did the carnivals, circuses, and fairs. He could fairly see the thousands of people strolling back and forth, listening to the raucous talk of the barkers in front of the ball games, bingo stands, grease joints, and other amusement contrivances of all sorts.

Jingle glanced idly at the bucking corral. There stood Dutch Oven, apart from the other horses, gazing wistfully across the arena as if he wished he were out there again. Something like sympathy filled Jingle's mind as he told himself: "It's only because man is the reason for his captivity that makes that critter so doggone mean. It's hardly fair to blame him. Sometimes horses are almost human."

Soft footsteps broke into his thoughts. Turning his head, he saw Many Beads, Two Crows' squaw, hurrying in pursuit of a tiny Indian boy, who was toddling toward the arena. Jingle grinned at the old squaw and shouted encouragement to the half-naked papoose.

Suddenly Jingle's heart skipped a beat, and a cold dampness rose on his brow. Eluding its mother, the youngster had just crawled under the bottom rail into the corral where Dutch Oven stood! Already the black stallion was glaring at the bronze child in the beaded leggings.

Swiftly Jingle leaped toward Many Beads and laid a hand on her shoulder to stop her frantic attempt to get into the corral. Trembling, sobbing, she turned and implored him in her native tongue. He looked through the rails. For the moment, the horse was retreating, uncertain how to deal with the strange little figure, but Jingle knew that as soon as the animal had backed into the far corner of the corral, he would strike.

Jingle edged forward and ducked through the rails slowly so as not to startle the stallion. If he could just get his hands on the kid! Each step sinking into the oozing mud, he cautiously approached the papoose. Behind him, shouts indicated aid was coming, but he knew it could not reach him in time. He stretched out his arm and took the hand of the child. Now the hard part was to move backward without letting the horse think he was showing fear. Meeting the glare of the stallion's blazing eyes squarely with his own, he began to back away; but Dutch Oven took a step forward! Feeling the fence at his back, Jingle glanced aside just long enough to see eager hands pull the little fellow through the barrier. In that second the stallion charged. As the dark form reared over him, and he caught for an agonized moment the glint of those dreaded flailing hooves, Jingle threw up an arm in self-defense. Then everything went black.

It seemed ages later as Jingle opened his eyes and a bright light nearly blinded him. After blinking a few times, he realized he lay in a snowy white bed and that a woman in a white uniform stood nearby smiling at him.

Jingle tried to move his head to look out the window, but as he did so, pain shot through his body, and he became aware of something hard around his arm and shoulder.

Then the nurse spoke: "You must be quiet. You were lucky enough to escape with only a broken shoulder. Now, if you feel up to it, there are some people out in the corridor who have been waiting for hours to see you."

By the light shining in the window, Jingle guessed it must be the morning after the day of the show. The door opened, and he saw his father come into the room. Crossing to the bed, Bill Laraday laid his hand on his son's head. For a long moment he stood gazing into Jingle's eyes.

"I hardly know what to say, Son," he said, "but

I'm sure proud of you. I never realized that you were practically grown to be a man. But things will be different from now on." Tears glistened in his eyes. It gave Jingle a funny feeling to see his father so deeply moved.

Again the door swung open. Two Crows stalked in, followed by Many Beads carrying her papoose. Forgetting for the moment the custom which forbade her walking in front of her husband, she ran to Jingle's side. Setting the child on the bed, she threw her arms around his rescuer. Jingle winced from the pain, and at a low word from Two Crows the squaw backed away.

Now the old chief advanced. In his hand he carried a beautifully engraved pair of riding boots. These he laid on the bed where Jingle could see them. Jingle noticed that the side of each boot bore a large "J" stamped on the leather, right above where his spurs would shine. But now the Indian began talking, so Jingle forced his eyes away from the wonderful boots and looked up at him.

"My people want you to have these. You are no longer a boy in our eyes. You are a man. You have saved the son of a chief, and he shall some day rule our tribe. Perhaps then he can tell you how my people love you."

When he had finished, Two Crows turned and quietly left the room. Many Beads and her son followed him. At the door she turned.

"I bring you good things to eat every day, Jinglespurs," she called.

Looking at his parent, Jingle found he couldn't

say anything. His father must have understood him for he said, "You'd better rest, Son. I've got to go and take care of Paint and Shotgun. Old Paint sure misses you. Won't hardly eat a bite. You better hurry and get well."

As the tall veteran rider left the room, Jingle somehow seemed to look right through the wall and see himself astride a plunging horse in front of a gaily colored mass of people who had gathered especially to watch the "World's Champion Bronc Rider."

although his mother had promised to feed Ba-ee,

Sagebrush Champion

HARRY SINCLAIR DRAGO

IT WAS their last run, and the band of desert broom-tails were making it a wild one. Two hundred strong, they poured down from the Paradise Road in a loose ball of dust and struck through the dwarf sage that carpets the long slope to the Humboldt River bottoms.

Eyes gleaming, wild as eagles, the sight of town and the railroad that was soon to carry them off to California, to be ground up into chicken feed, seemed to fill them with a last desperate resolve to break free. Time after time, they whirled and headed back for the road, manes flattened and tails flying in the morning breeze. Always the six men who had hazed them in from the far reaches of the Owyhee Desert were ahead of them and turned them back.

This herd of wild horses represented three months' work. Owyhee Bill Ryan and the men who rode with him weren't losing any now if they could help it. At eight dollars a head, they had sixteen hundred dollars staring them in the face. Split six ways, it was only wages—wages earned the hard way.

The shrill cries of the men, the screaming of the frightened ponies and the swelling cloud of dust had not gone unnoticed in Winnemucca. Old-timers, who could remember when the big beef herds had come pounding down off the Paradise Road, quickened their step and started for the railroad corrals beside the Western Pacific tracks. Those beef herds didn't come any more; sheep had this country by the throat now. So it was something to see just a bunch of broom-tails high tailing it through the brush.

But it wasn't only the old-timers whose interest had been captured by sight of the *caballada.* Up the river a few hundred yards from the town bridge that crosses the Humboldt at the W. P. station, there was a cabin, made of discarded railroad ties, that stood half hidden in the willow brakes along the bank.

Standing in the doorway, a slow anger and bitter resentment building up in him, was Johnnie Colpitt. He had been watching the horse herd almost from the moment it hove into sight.

Johnnie was only a kid; in fact, he was called the Kid, or when that was not definite enough, the Paradise Kid. Those big herds which once had come bawling down from the North—those flush days when northern Nevada was booming cattle country—had been before his time. In him there was only the memory of lean pickings on this range, of more and more Basque sheepmen, of the burred broncho grass killing off the grama, of dry farmers, of dwindling herds and fewer and fewer jobs.

What the end was to be, he didn't know, but sight of these luckless broom-tails going to their ignominious end came close to giving him the answer. His thin young face corded with bitterness, he stood there until the herd had swept by. He knew Owyhee Bill, Joe Rust and the others. He didn't hold against them what they were doing. In these times, a man had to make a dollar whatever way he could. But these ponies were wild things; one of the few wild things left in this country. And because the Kid loved horses, it was too much for him.

"They weren't harmin' no one," he muttered as he stepped back into the darkened cabin where a gaunt old man, half blind with cataracts, sat rocking endlessly. "If this keeps up, might as well turn the country over to the sheepmen and be done with it."

Anse Colpitt shook his head patiently. "No use takin' on thataway, Son. Them hosses ain't wuth nuthin'. All runty with inbreedin.' Hooves so soft from drinkin' alkali water you couldn't git a shoe to stick on one in ten."

"What of it?" the Kid demanded. "You don't have to grind 'em up into chicken meat."

The old man nodded dully. "Use to be lots of 'em around; wild hosses was everywhere when I fust come to Paradise Valley," he said. "Once in a while you could trap a good one. Made a fair-to-middlin' cow pony. That was before yore time, Johnnie."

The boy clamped on his hat. He stopped in the doorway. "Purty bright out," he remarked. "You stay inside today, Dad. Your eyes botherin' you much this mornin'?"

" 'Bout as usual."

"Hope I can git you down to Frisco before winter," the Kid told him. "A good doctor down there could fix you up."

"Where you goin' now?" his father asked.

"Into town. I'll git your tobacco. Guess I'll drop over to the corrals before I come back; I'd like to see this stuff."

He struck off down the river path with a free-swinging stride, lean, narrow-hipped and straight as an arrow. In the free and easy way of a little desert town, folks knew how things were with him and often wondered how he got by. Everyone wondered what old Anse Colpitt would have done without him. But that wasn't their only reason for liking the Kid; he was a good worker and always ready to try his hand at any job that offered.

Buck Ransford, the tall, grizzled sheriff of Humboldt Country, jerked a friendly nod at the youth as they passed on Bridge Street. "Mawnin', Kid," he said. "Figgered you'd be down to the tracks by now."

"Got to git some tobacco for the old man first," the Kid replied. "By the way, Buck, you ain't heard of no one lookin' for a man, have yuh?"

"No, but somethin' will be turnin' up soon,"

Ransford told him. "Others waitin' and hopin' too." With a little jerk of his head he indicated several punchers roosting on the low cement step in front of the Gem Saloon. "Cowboys without horses," he murmured more to himself than the Kid. "Too bad! Well, fall's comin' and things will pick up about rodeo time. I suppose you'll be ridin' Slash Decker's Piute Chief in the races again this year."

"Not after what happened last week," the Kid said flatly. Buck Ransford smiled tolerantly at his vehemence.

"You shouldn't hold it against Slash that he had to let you go last week," he counseled. "When business is bad, a man's got to cut down. Slash ain't been averagin' better than two freightin' outfits a day at Toll House of late. No one usin' the road. Wasn't much use of keepin' a stock-tender out there."

"Buck, you got it wrong," the kid declared. "Slash didn't fire me 'cause business was bad. I caught him sluggin' a horse an' told him what I thought about it. He got sore."

"Yeah?" The sheriff gazed at him shrewdly. "Guess Decker ain't holdin' it against you. I was talkin' to him this mornin'. He said he figgered you'd be ridin' for him at the show."

"He did?" the Kid grunted, surprised. "Well, he's foolin' himself. If he's goin' to win the race again this year, he'll have to get somebody else to do his ridin', much as I need the money."

A narrow plank walk topped the high fences that formed the walls of the shipping pens on the

W. P. siding. When the Kid arrived he found a score of men there watching the milling horses. He climbed up with the others.

Seen at close range, these broom-tails were a runty lot, short-necked, their heads too big for their bodies.

"Pop was right. They don't amount to much," the Kid thought. "But they're horses. They didn't have this comin' to 'em."

In the next to the last pen a big spirited buckskin stallion caught his eye. The horse was a good three hands higher than any other animal in the corrals.

"Nothin' runty about him," the Kid thought, sizing up the horse with an almost professional eye. "Good long barrel on him. Nice chest, too. Clean a pair of legs as ever you'd want to see!"

The Kid sat down on the plank walk and studied the animal, ignoring the rest of the bunch. The big buckskin was fighting mad. Squealing with rage, it reared up on its hind legs and tried to leap over the high fence.

Failing in that, it attacked the fence first with its hind legs and then with its fore, trying in vain to kick the pen to pieces. The Kid held his breath as he saw the horse back off from the fence, head stretched out, nostrils distended, eyes rolling with fury, and then hurl itself at the wooden barrier, crashing into it with such force that a board snapped. It brought Owyhee Bill Ryan on the run. He waved a coiled rope at the big horse and cursed it to a finish. The sight of the rope seemed to strike fear in the stallion. It backed off, trembling, its lips turned back from its teeth.

Turning, Owyhee Bill saw the Kid. He called a greeting.

"That buckskin is the orneriest one in the bunch," he declared, wiping his brow on his sleeve. "Raised the devil ever since we trapped him. Ain't you out to Toll House no more, Kid?"

"Got through Saturday."

"So? Heard things is awful quiet. Suppose yo're waitin' for the rodeo to come along."

"Don't know about that," the Kid volunteered. "I ain't ridin' Decker's horse."

Owyhee was curious. He got such details as the Kid was willing to give. There was a heavy-footed humor of a sort in the mustanger. He resorted to it now.

"If you could break that big buckskin, Kid," he suggested, "you wouldn't have to worry about Slash Decker's horse. That big fella would make that bronc of Decker's think it was goin' backward. Yes, sir! You could make yoreself some real jack with that critter."

"Looks like he could go all right," the Kid agreed admiringly. "He took my eye right off."

"Waal, I'll let you have him cheap—eight bucks," Owyhee offered solemnly. It was cruel in a way; he knew the Kid didn't have eight dollars to spare. "That buckskin's never been branded. I'd give you a bill of sale that would sure enough make him yours. That prize money counts up to two hundred dollars. It would set you right up in business."

He was putting it on pretty thick, but the Kid was too taken with the horse to be suspicious. "I sure'd like to have him," he murmured. "Reckon I could gentle him all right. I kind o' got a way with horses. You let me think it over for an hour, Owyhee."

The mustanger relented at that. He had hardly expected the boy to take him so seriously. "I was just kiddin'," he grinned. "I wouldn't sell you that hell cat, Kid. He's an outlaw, broke away from some ranch. He'd kill you if you ever tried to put a saddle on him."

He lost his grin abruptly when the Kid said, "I wouldn't care about him bein' an outlaw. I just want to do a little figgerin' on the eight dollars. I'll be back directly."

Owyhee stared at the Kid, amazed, as he slid off the walk and started for town, his stride longer than usual and every line of him sharp with determination.

"I don't know whether he can run or not," the Kid told himself, "but they ain't goin' to cut him up into chicken meat—not if I got to eat oatmeal all winter!"

"You earn the money, so I reckon it's up to you to say how it'll be spent," his father said, when the Kid asked his advice. "If yo're set on it, you better git him. If you can't break him, and he turns out to be a good bucker, I reckon Burrell might buy him for his string when he comes up to the rodeo."

"I'll never sell this fella," the Kid insisted.

"Guess I'll have chances aplenty," he added confidently.

There was good grass on the flats along the river. The Kid put the big buckskin on it at the end of a picket rope. No one ever went down that way. That was what the Kid wanted. The big horse was as wild as Owyhee had said he was, and being left to himself was the best medicine for him.

"I don't want no one to go near him or try to lay a hand on him but me," the Kid told his father. "I gotta show him he's got nothin' to be afraid of. I never make a quick move when I'm near him. He's got a lot of savvy in him. Give him a chance to figger things out and he'll come around."

The days went by. No job was offered, and the Kid was too engrossed with the horse to worry about it. From discarded lumber, he made a stable for the buckskin.

One evening he inched along the picket rope and actually put his hand on the animal's muzzle. The horse trembled under his touch but did not bolt. It was the beginning of a strange surrender.

"Gosh, you're a beauty," the Kid glowed. "One of these days I'm goin' to put a saddle on you."

It came sooner than he expected. Every evening for a week he led the horse around before he attempted to mount him. The first ride was a dizzy one, but the Kid stayed with him; he knew how much depended on it. Let a horse know he can buck off a man and he'll often never be satisfied with anything less.

Finally the stallion straightened out and began

to run. A dirt road ran from town to the Rinehart Dam, up the river. Save for the town boys who went up to the dam to swim in the evening, there was seldom anyone on the road. The Kid put the big horse over it.

"Man, can you travel!" he exulted. "Git a little grain into you and there ain't no cold-blooded horse in this country can stay with you!"

The stallion was in a lather when the Kid got him back to the stable. He walked him until he cooled him off, then rubbed him down affectionately in the early dark, talking to him as he worked.

"You ain't no shucks as a bucker," he murmured. "Purty fancy crowhopper. There's too much civilized horse blood in you for you to be a bucker."

The stallion took a lump of sugar from the Kid's hand. The Kid's arm stole around the arched neck. He had had few things to love in his life, and all the affection in him went out to the horse.

"Got to have a name for you, fella," he whispered. "You're goin' to be a champion. Gee, that's what I'm goin' to call you! Champ! That's your name!"

It became the order of things for the Kid to put the big horse over the dirt road to the dam every evening after the sun had dropped below the Sonoma Peaks. The news trickled into town. One night the Kid found Sheriff Buck Ransford waiting for him at the cabin. He was instantly fearful that Buck had come about Champ.

"No, Kid," Ransford laughed. "Owyhee told me

all about it. I was watchin' you this evenin'. That big fella can sure pack the mail."

"Yeah, he can step some." The Kid grinned. "Don't skeer so easy at sight of folks no more. But no one 'cept me better ever try to put a hand on him."

Ransford winked at the old man. "Anse, the boy's got a bee buzzin' in his head. I know what he's thinkin' just as plain as though he'd told me."

The Kid's grin was sheepish. "Reckon there's no foolin' you, Buck. You really think he's purty fast, eh?"

"Plenty!" the sheriff nodded. "We'll measure off a half mile on the road and I'll show up with a stop watch one of these evenin's. We know what Piute Chief's time was last year. We'll see how yore fella can measure up to that."

They timed the big horse four nights running. He never equaled Piute Chief's mark, but he showed more than enough speed to send the Kid's hopes soaring.

"He'll be seven-eight seconds faster on a track," he told the sheriff.

"Ought to be that much difference," Buck agreed. "Maybe I can fix it so you can work him out at the rodeo track. I'll speak to Carl about it. In the meantime, you ought to grain him a little. He sweats awful easy."

"I'd like to put him on hard grain, Buck," the Kid said hesitatingly. "Don't see how I can scrape up the money, though."

"Well, maybe I'll take a little flyer with you and go to bat for a few bushels of oats—"

"I ain't lookin' for no charity," the Kid cut him off.

"No charity about it," Buck said thoughtfully. "I like this big horse. And as for you, you've always been a good boy, Johnnie. You've got a little break comin' to you. The rodeo is a month away, and a lot of things can happen in that time."

Buck meant that a lot of pleasant things could happen; but other things could happen, too. He was not the only man in Winnemucca who got into the habit of slipping out on the Rinehart road of an evening to watch the Champ's workouts. The Kid had never felt so important.

He was skimping along on little or nothing a day, but he was happier than he had ever believed he could be. His pride in Champ was matched only by his love for the big horse. Dreaming one night that some one had taken the horse away from him, he woke up in a cold sweat and raced out to the stable.

Champ was there, safe and sound, and the Kid was so overcome with relief that he failed to regard the dream as an ill omen. Trouble was marching at him, however.

There was legalized gambling in Winnemucca. Silver Tremaine, who ran the games at the hotel, heard enough about the Kid and his horse to repeat the story to his friend, Slash Decker. Slash, a violent man, heavy-set and with a rocky face that might have been carved out of granite, refused to take the big buckskin as a serious competitor of his own Piute Chief.

"Some folks in this town think he's got a chance —Buck Ransford, for one," Silver told him. "They'll stake the Kid to the entrance money."

"Ain't no horse in these parts can beat the Chief!" Decker insisted belligerently. "We've always cleaned up on him, ain't we?"

"With the Kid riding him," said Tremaine. He had a chilling way of making a point. He was contemptuous of Decker's mental processes and at times did not bother to conceal the fact. "It may dawn on you eventually that you ain't got nobody to ride the Chief. I don't care about this horse the Kid's got, but I know doggone well that he can't ride two horses in the same race."

"Why, he can't throw me down like that!" Decker growled.

"Can't he?" was the cynical query. "I don't know what *he* can do, but I can tell you what you're going to do. You're going to make certain if he rides in that race, he rides for you."

Decker's blue eyes narrowed and his face was suddenly as rocky as Gibraltar. He was a brutal, mean-souled man, but essentially honest. The success of his horse had given him a prominence that was the most precious thing in his drab life. It didn't matter that the second-rate thoroughbreds that were brought up from the coast for the rodeo were faster; it was enough for him to be pointed out as the owner of the best cold-blooded horse in the county.

Tremaine knew his man; knew that Slash would go a long way to keep himself on top. And he had a hold on Decker; it was his money that backed Piute Chief.

"You suggestin' that I git the Kid's horse out of the way?" Decker demanded bluntly.

"I ain't suggesting nothing—though you may have a good idea there at that. Just make sure that the Kid rides your horse. We'll go out there tonight and see him run this buckskin."

One look at Champ and Decker got as pale as a ghost.

"Fast, eh?" Tremaine laughed unpleasantly, ignorant of what was boiling in Decker. "You're taking him seriously enough now, ain't you?"

"Silver—I know that horse!" Slash blurted. "I know them markin's—them long legs! I can't be mistaken! That big devil is the buckskin that broke away from Charlie Twist's ranch two years ago!"

It was Tremaine's turn to be surprised. "You sure?" he whipped out.

"Positive!" Decker mopped his brow, his shrewd little brain working furiously. "I got my cue now," he growled. "The Kid won't have that horse long!"

Three mornings later, Buck Ransford, Charlie Twist and two of his punchers, and Slash Decker arrived at the Kid's cabin.

"Kid, it breaks my heart to have to do this, but I got to take Champ away from you," Ransford announced heavily.

"You what?" the Kid gasped.

"I got a court order to turn the horse over to Charlie. Seems it belongs to him. He went before the judge with his witnesses and proved it."

The Kid's face was gray. "Buck, you can't do this! You know I bought Champ! He ain't got no brand on him—"

"No brand on him, but he's mine," old Charlie put in. He didn't appear any too happy about this business. He had no use for Slash Decker, but an outlaw horse that had been broken to saddle was worth money. The horse being his, he wanted it. "A man puts a brand on his stuff for his convenience. He don't have to brand it."

"That's right, Kid," Buck muttered.

The Kid's eyes went to Decker. "What are you doin' here?" he demanded.

"I want to talk to you, Kid, when you git through with these men."

"My boy's honest!" Anse Colpitt yelled from the doorway.

" 'Course he is," said Ransford. "You keep back out of the light, Anse. I'll look out for the boy."

"I don't suppose you know anythin' about this." The Kid spoke bitterly to Decker. "I'll bet I can thank *you* for it. And you can take your talk to somebody that wants to hear it! I don't!"

"There's one thing you can do, Kid," Ransford suggested. "You can put a lien on Champ. He was runnin' wild. You bought him from the man who captured him. You've broke him and you've fed him. I reckon the court will figger you got a bill of about seventy-five dollars against him."

"It ain't up to you to be suggestin' things like that," Decker jerked out angrily.

"I'm doin' it just the same," was Buck's quiet answer.

"Waal, I don't figger I ought to be made to buy back my own horse," said Old Charlie. "He ain't wuth seventy-five, or even fifty—"

"He is if he can win the cold-blooded race," Ransford interrupted.

"Race?" Twist exclaimed blankly. "Decker didn't tell me the Paradise Kid was figgerin' to race him."

"Didn't he? Just what did Slash tell you, Charlie?"

"He told me the Kid had my horse; that he'd broke him. Times bein' what they are, I figgered it was wuth lookin' into. Why didn't *you* tell me about this before, Buck?"

"I thought it would be better to wait until we all got together," Ransford answered evenly. "It's a purty rotten deal to hand a boy—especially a boy that's a square-shooter and never had any breaks."

The Kid had walked up to Decker, his face bloodless.

"So it was you!" he cried. "I knew it!"

"Just a minit!" old Charlie broke in. He was well along in his sixties, and thin to emaciation, but there was plenty of fight in him. He raised a clenched fist to Slash. "Dang yore mean carcass, just what was yore game in comin' to me?"

"No game," Slash said uncomfortably. "I thought—"

"What you thought was that you could kill two birds with one stone," the sheriff finished for him. "If you could get Charlie to take Champ back to his spread on Happy Creek, your horse wouldn't have him to beat, and you'd be all set to wear the Kid down into ridin' the Chief."

"Well, by gravy, that game is goin' to backfire on you, Decker!" old Charlie snorted. "I'm gittin' interested!" He pulled out his wallet and peeled off some bills. "Kid, I'm giving you fifty dollars for your bill. You ride the horse in the race and we'll split the purse even up!"

The Kid shook his head. He was near to tears and his quivering chin gave him away. "I don't want the money. I want Champ. He's . . . he's all I got—"

Ransford put his arm around him. "The rest of you stay here. Me and the Kid are goin' to walk down to the stable." Once out of sight of the others, Buck said, "I know just how you feel, Kid. I thought you was goin' to bust down, back there. I wouldn't have blamed you. You been awful game about his."

A sob shook the boy. "I never figgered nothin' like this would happen—"

"Mebbe it's better it did," Buck declared soberly. "I got an idea everythin's goin' to work out all right. But you got to play ball with old Charlie. He's makin' you a good proposition. You take his fifty dollars. It'll help out, comin' now, and you won't have to be worryin' about your father. Then you win this race. After it's all over, I'm thinkin' you'll be able to buy Champ back."

"You mean that, Buck?" the Kid asked, his face alight with desperate earnestness.

"I do. Charlie'll know by then that Champ won't let no one but you ride him, won't he?"

It satisfied the Kid. "O. K.," he said. "You go back and tell him. And get Decker away from here. I'll use a stock whip on him if you don't, Buck!"

"He'll go," Ransford promised.

As usual, the Kid arranged to have Peewee Roberts look after his father while he was away. With nearly three weeks to go until the day of the race, old Charlie insisted on taking the Champ out to Happy Creek.

"You can work him out without no one keepin' cases on you," he told the Kid. "No sense in lettin' anyone but ourselves know just how good he is."

By early afternoon he and his punchers and the Kid were ready to leave. Ransford took Charlie aside for a word or two.

"Keep an eye on the horse and on the Kid," he advised. "There's always a lot of money bet on this race. Silver Tremaine is behind Decker. He'll bear watchin'. If somethin' happens to Champ or the Kid at the last minute, it would be awfully convenient for certain parties."

"Just let 'em try anythin' like that and we'll need you and the coroner in yore professional capacities on Happy Creek," the old man assured him.

Buck Ransford was an astute man. Little happened in town that he didn't digest thoroughly. As a rule, he came up with the right answer. As rodeo week neared, he became particularly interested in the betting odds. Piute Chief was the favorite.

Decker had got a young half-breed from the McDermitt reservation to ride his horse. The boy was well known in town, and for two years running had ridden horses that had finished second. Some money was being wagered on a Paradise Valley horse. But if a single bet had been made on the Champ, Buck failed to hear about it.

"The situation is just about what it ought to be," he told himself. "Mebbe I was wrong in figgerin' that Tremaine might try to put the Kid and his horse out of the race."

Then the odds lengthened. Tremaine made the Chief a five-to-three favorite. It didn't make sense to Ransford.

"Champ's too good a horse for that," he thought. "And Silver's too smart to git out on the end of that kind of a limb without havin' somethin' up his sleeve."

Buck worried about it for a day and then found an excuse that took him to Happy Creek. What he found there reassured him; the Kid was smiling again and the big horse was getting faster every day.

"Never knew they was so much fun hereabouts," old Charlie cackled enthusiastically.

"They're bettin' five to three that you won't win," Buck told him. "I don't like it."

"I'll take five hundred of that!" the old man declared without hesitation. "I'll give you the money. You put it up when you get back."

"All right, if you say so," Buck agreed reluctantly. "But I'm tellin' you to look out for a trick. They're goin' to try to pull somethin'. The odds ain't honest, Charlie."

"Well, we're ready for anythin' they pull!" the old man declared furiously. "We're purty near sleepin' and eatin' with that horse."

Ransford expected the bet he made for Twist to have some effect on the odds. But nothing happened. Friends asked him about the Champ. He told them what he knew. Many of them put down wagers. Still the odds remained at five to three.

The rodeo was a three-day affair. As time for it neared, Winnemucca began to liven up. Strings of lights were strung across Bridge Street. The saloons did a booming business. Flags and bunting appeared. The fact that it had been another bad year on the range was forgotten temporarily. The fair grounds west of town were shining with new paint. Strangers were drifting in; rodeo riders from the last show at Burns, Oregon; bulldoggers, cowgirls, ropers.

Slash Decker brought in Piute Chief and saw him established in one of the long row of stables on the rodeo grounds. Other horses were there already, thoroughbreds and range stock, the stalls of the latter swarming with punchers and cowmen, their conversation horsy and colored to suit the occasion.

The Kid and Charlie Twist, accompanied by his whole outfit, hit town the day before the race. The Champ was immediately taken to the rodeo grounds and stabled. When the Kid headed for home to see his father, Ransford made it his business to accompany him.

"Stickin' purty close to me, aren't you, Buck," the Kid laughed.

"I aim to," was the sober answer. "You're not goin' to turn up missin' tomorrow if I can help it. I know Champ is all right with Charlie's crew stayin' with him."

He said as much to Anse Colpitt half an hour later. "Just to be sure that nothin' goes wrong," he added, "I want the Kid to sleep at the jail tonight. Either me or Early Proust will be there."

For the rest of the day, Buck didn't let the Kid out of his sight. When night came, he fixed up a bunk in one of the cells for him. "You can amuse yourself here in the office till you're ready to turn in," he told him. "I'll stick around until midnight; Early will drop in then."

It was the big night of the year down on Bridge Street. On the lawn beside the Nixon Opera House the band was giving a concert. The Kid could hear the music, sour notes and all. About ten o'clock old Charlie walked into the sheriff's office.

"Big doin's," he declared.

"Your crew is keepin' out of it, I hope," said Buck.

"Pete Ambers and my foreman, Lin Evans, are," Charlie assured him. "Lin has a hundred bucks up on Champ to win. A mouse couldn't get in that stable without him knowin' it."

He didn't stay long. "I'm goin' to turn in, Kid," he said. "You ought to do the same."

"I'm doin' it right now," the Kid assured him. "Tomorrow is goin' to be a long day."

Save for Pete Dolores, who was awaiting trial for having made some permanent changes in one of his countrymen with a knife, the Kid had the cell block to himself. Pete called out a pleasant good night.

The Kid had been asleep almost three hours when he heard Pete calling to him. "Keed, wake up!" the prisoner shouted. "There ees beeg fire at the rodeo grounds!"

The Kid leaped out of bed and ran to the barred window. Over toward the fair grounds the sky was stained a bright crimson. The sight wrung a groan out of him. In a second, he had pulled on his overalls and slipped into his boots. On the dead run he raced through the office and knocked Deputy Proust aside. Deaf to the latter's plea to come back, he sped up the street and cut through the vacant lots in the direction of the fire. In a few minutes he saw that it was the rodeo stables that were afire.

"My God!" he groaned, thinking of Champ. "They're bone-dry! They'll go up like tinder!"

It was almost a mile from the jail to the stables. Desperation lent speed to his legs and strength to his lungs. Others were running to the fire. He passed a dozen. Knocking a man out of his path, he darted through the gate and started for Champ's stable. Before he was halfway down the line, Lin Evans, old Charlie's foreman, grabbed him.

"It's all right, Kid!" Lin cried. "I moved Champ down here on a hunch 'bout an hour ago! He's O. K.! There he is, down by the track, with Ambers and the boys!"

Along the row of stables men were trying to get the frightened horses out and having a bad time of it.

"Looks like it started at the end where Champ was," the Kid gasped breathlessly.

"Sure did!" said Evans. "This fire was set!"

Buck Ransford arrived on a borrowed horse a few moments later. Old Charlie was just behind, his shirt tail flapping unnoticed in the night breeze.

"Guess I had it right all along," Buck muttered when he had heard the facts.

By now the fire was burning fiercely. Already it had consumed seven or eight stalls. Fifty yards away, Slash Decker's angry bellowing rose above the crackling of the flames.

"That's Decker," the Kid cried.

Ransford ran up to Slash. At sight of him, Decker's wrath found a specific objective. "Damn you bunglin' politicians!" he cried. "No protection! No water line out here! Nothin'!" He wrung his hands in his impotence. "My horse is a goner!"

"You should have thought of these things, Decker," Ransford declared. His meaning was clear.

The Kid had taken a look at the fire and whirled on old Charlie. "Yank off that shirt and give it to me!" he cried.

"Kid, what are you goin' to do?" Charlie demanded, bewildered.

"I'm goin' to get the Chief out of there! He knows me! I can handle him!"

"Kid, yo're crazy!" the old man yelled. "You know what these skunks tried to do to us!"

"I can't help it! I can't let that horse die like that!"

He ripped the shirt in two and doused it in a bucket of water that was being passed up to the fire. Tying a piece of it around his head, up to his eyes, he dashed into the blazing stall.

In the lurid light of the flames he could see the terror-stricken horse, forelegs planted wide, staring at him with fear-crazed eyes.

He spoke soothingly to the horse, got its halter free and tried to drag him toward the gate. The roof was blazing. The animal squealed as a burning board fell across its withers. The Kid hastily knocked the board to the ground. His lungs were filling with smoke. He knew he couldn't stay there long and live. Flames from loose hay on the stall floor began to lick his legs.

"Chief, it's now or never!" he cried. He managed to get the wet shirt over the horse's head, but as the cloth touched its eyes the animal reared wildly. The Kid managed to stay with him. One hand holding the wet rag in place, he grabbed Piute's mane and started to swing himself up. Before he could make it the whole rear end of the roof came crashing down. Hands and legs burned, the smoke smothering him, he tried to mount again, and this time he made it.

With spurs digging into his sides, the Chief came plunging out of the stable with a rush that scattered the onlookers right and left.

Ransford lifted the Kid down as Charlie and a score of men came running up.

"Kid, are you all right?" Buck asked anxiously. He was proud of this youngster.

"Sure. Got a few burns, but I'm O. K."

"You are not!" Charlie got out excitedly. "Look at them hands! Where's a doctor?" he bellowed at the crowd. "Where's Doc Giroux? Make the Kid lie down, Buck! We'll get a rig—get him to the hospital!"

Decker came up to grumble his thanks. Ransford waved him away. "This was a kindness to a horse, Decker—not to you."

The Kid spent the rest of the night in the county hospital. In the early morning, Buck and old Charlie came into his room with little Doc Giroux.

"How you feelin'?" Buck asked at once.

The Kid managed a smile. "Purty good," he said.

"Doc says you'll be in bed a day or two," Twist returned. "I tried to get the race postponed till the last day of the show. Decker wouldn't consent to it. The dirty skunks did their damnedest to put our horse out of the race, and now they're just as well satisfied because you can't ride. It means a sure thing for 'em, the low-down double-crossers!"

Buck Ransford was watching the Kid. He saw the boy's jaws tighten. "Bigger things than a horse race sometimes," the sheriff observed consolingly. "You showed this country somethin' last night, Kid."

"I'll show 'em somethin' today, too; I'm ridin' that race! I know lots of folks has bet on Champ. I can't let 'em down."

"I had a hunch you'd feel that way," Ransford nodded. He turned to the doctor. "Can he make it, doc?"

"He shouldn't try it," said Giroux. "He'll be back here for two weeks if he does."

"And we'll break his heart if we keep him out of the race." Ransford shook his head.

"You try to keep me out of it!" the Kid warned them. "I'm ridin'!"

"Yeah, I guess that's the way it will be," Ransford nodded. "Seems when you got sand enough in you, you can do most anythin'."

The noise of the crowd, the blaring of the band and excitement of the few minutes just before the race reached the Kid only vaguely as Lin Evans and Ransford lifted him into the saddle. Old Charlie groaned to himself as he saw the Kid eye his heavily swathed hands with a thoughtful expression.

"Kid, I ain't goin' to tell you how to ride your race," he said. "Just remember you got a big, powerful horse under you and that you can't fight him with yore hurt hands."

"I'll be all right," the Kid murmured grimly. "Champ is actin' like a gentleman. This distance ain't nothin' for him. If I can get him ahead, I'm goin' to stay up there all the way around."

Ransford walked beside the Champ as Lin led the horse to the barrier, in this case just a rope stretched across the track. "I ain't got a cent on this race," he told the boy, "but it couldn't mean more to me if you were ridin' for me. I know you're doin' this on your nerve. I saw how you looked when you picked up the rein. Guess your legs is purty bad, too, they way you're tryin' to keep 'em away from the saddle skirts."

"I'll make it, Buck," the kid declared, his face pinched and white.

With daggers of pain shooting through his arms, the Kid lifted the big horse as the rope fell. Champ got away clean. There were five horses in the race, but by the time the big buckskin flashed by the first pole only Piute Chief was with him.

The two horses stuck together as they tore down the back stretch. The Kid knew the Chief was strong and game. "I got to lose him here," he gritted. "Can't wait until we're in the stretch."

The blisters on his legs had broken already. He could feel the water from them seeping down his limbs. Biting his tongue at the raw torture of it, he drove his knees into Champ and felt the big horse respond with a fresh burst of speed. Daylight began to show between the two horses. But Piute Chief was not beaten yet.

Suddenly the home stretch opened before them. The crowd was on its feet, shouting itself hoarse. That wall of noise seemed to throw the Champ out of stride. He started to swing wide. His senses reeling with agony, the Kid clamped down on the rein and straightened him out.

All the way to the wire it was a slashing, driving ride. Piute Chief came up once, only to fall back. The Kid was beyond doing anything but clinging to his saddle now. He knew he couldn't stick to it much longer. His head was spinning; his pain-racked flesh defying his will to make it endure more.

"I got to stick," he muttered. "I got to stick!"

Then he saw the wire! He was under it! He had won! He didn't hear the cheer that went up for him. With his last conscious breath he kicked his feet out of the stirrups and pitched into the dust.

Ransford was sitting at his bedside in the hospital when the Kid opened his eyes that evening. They gazed at each other a long time before either spoke.

"I told you I'd make it," the Kid murmured.

Buck nodded. "I'd hate to own anythin' you wanted real bad. I reckon you'd manage to git it."

"Charlie been around?" the boy asked.

"Yeah, just stepped out for a minute."

The old man came in a little later. He grinned at the Kid. "Comin' around all right, eh? Well, you take it easy. Stay here as long as you want; I've taken care of everythin'. Buck tell you that Silver Tremaine has left town? No? Well he did. Cleaned out of everythin', I understand."

Charlie took an envelope from his pocket and

tossed it on the bed. "I'm headin' back to the creek early in the mornin'," he said casually. "You'll find yore money in there. When yo're ready to go to work, come out. I'll have a job for you."

"Gee, Charlie, you certainly been swell about everythin'," the Kid declared tremulously. "I'll be able to do somethin' for my father's eyes now. You sure been swell to me."

"You been purty swell yoreself." The old man swallowed hard and turned away. "I'll be seein' you," he said as he walked out.

Ransford picked up the envelope. "A hundred dollars here, Kid," he said. "And a paper. Want me to read it to you?"

"Sure."

"It says, 'For the sum of one dollar and other valuable considerations, hereby acknowledged, I sell to Johnnie Colpitt my horse known as the Champ.' "

It took the Kid a few moments to get the full meaning of it. "Gee, gosh!" he gasped in wide-eyed delight. "I didn't expect this! Why, that says Champ is mine. He belongs to me!"

"That's what it says, Kid." Ransford blew his nose noisily. "I reckon that's the way it ought to be."

A Horse of Her Own

STEPHEN PAYNE

RIDING double behind Brother Bill to school, Mary said, "How I wish I had a horse of my very own!"

"Me too," agreed Bill. "But not half as much as I wish I had a good saddle."

"That's what he always says," thought Mary. "And he's never offered to help me buy a pony either . . . 'A good saddle!' I'm satisfied to ride bareback!"

Until last summer, it hadn't particularly mattered that she must ride double with Bill. Then all at once, because she was growing up, it mattered so terribly much, that Mary asked Daddy to help her out although she didn't really expect he could. She understood how hard up were Daddy and Mother Phillips on the small L 7 Ranch in the High Rockies.

Excepting the blue overalls she wore when riding and choring, Mother made all of Mary's clothes out of scraps. And not in three years had Mother had a new dress.

When Daddy said he could not buy a pony for her, Mary had started to sell blueing. If she sold eighteen packages for ten cents each and sent the money to the blueing company, she would receive a watch as a premium.

Disposing of her entire stock was up-hill work, but at last Mary received the wonderful watch. It was shiny, very thick and heavy and its back cover had to be pried off to get at the knobs for winding and setting it. All the boys in school wanted it until Chet Reardon sneered, "Cheap junk! 'Tain't a watch. It's a clock!"

But in spite of Chet, Business Woman Mary had sold the watch to Ted Livingston for one whole dollar! Since then she had added to this first dollar all other money she was able to earn.

On this bright June morning the meadow larks were singing and the prairie dogs and gophers in the sage brush along the road seemed as happy as the songsters. Distant blue-green mountains lifted white-capped peaks into the blue sky, and the nearer hills were softly green and beautiful.

But today Mary saw none of this beauty. Could she ever get a pony for herself? . . . All at once came an idea: Why not ask Don Murphy to help her.

Don, a dark boy, older than Mary, had great brown eyes which could dance with fun. Yet Mary had found him shy, silent, and somehow mysterious, because Don's father was a mustanger. Everyone, even his son, called him "Mustang," for he made his living by catching wild horses.

A flame of excitement ran through Mary's nerves when she saw Don's buckskin horse already picketed below the hill on which stood the log schoolhouse. How fortunate that she and Bill were early this morning!

Leaving Bill to stake out old Pete, Mary ran up the hill and pretended great surprise when she found the tall, dark-eyed boy in the schoolroom. Don hadn't been to school a great deal, so he was now trying to catch up in his classes.

Mary hung her hat on a nail, took her courage in both hands and walked over to his desk. "Don, there's something I must talk to you about!"

His tanned face began to redden and she wondered why any boy should be so bashful with a girl. In that drawly voice she loved to hear he said, "I don't know how to talk to girls."

"Never mind . . . Your father always has horses to sell or trade?"

"Sure."

"Well, I'd—I'd like to buy a little pony, my size. A coal black one."

"Mustang's got just the horse you want." Don's eyes lighted. His embarrassment was suddenly gone.

"Oh, Don, that's swell. But how—how much—?"

"He sells 'em for a song, Mary. You know mustangs ain't worth much. He'll take ten bucks for Torchy."

"Ten bucks!" Mary's hopes went down, down, down.

However, she had stirred Don's interest and sympathy. "Seems like a lot—to us," he said. "But," a grin ran across his face, "if a buyer raises half, Mustang'll trust him for the rest . . . I broke Torchy to ride bareback. I'd like you to get him!"

"Bareback? That's the way I ride." A new and wonderful emotion tingled Mary's nerves. Don would like her to get Torchy!

Impulsively she reached into her overalls pocket for her note book. "I'm going to show you how I've been saving to buy a pony. It's something like a diary, too, and no one's seen it. You won't make fun of me, will you, Don?"

" 'Course not. Mustang's learned—taught—me that girls and women—how to treat them, I mean."

Though she was feeling strangely self-conscious, Mary's bright head was close to his as they read the note book items:

"$1.00 . . For watch from blueing I sold.
Folks told me blueing no good and not to try to sell them more. Was I let down!

.50 . . For young magpie I sold to Mr. Barlow.
He wanted to see if he could make it talk. But it never did though I snagged my shirt and overalls getting it.

.60 . . For wild raspberries I peddled.
Jessie Lyons went with me double

on her horse to pick them behind the sandhills. She ate all she picked and got awful sick. I pretty near didn't get her home 'cause a bear scared her horse and it pulled loose and ran away. So'd the bear.

.10 . . For cap I knitted stage-driver Jack McQuire.

Jack paid me $.90 but the yarn from the big mail order catalog cost $.80 postage paid. Jack says the cap's dandy. But why don't he ever wear it?

1.00 . . For feeding Mr. Reardon's dogie calf warm milk and keeping it alive.

He's rich, a big cowman, but he wouldn't give me the calf after I found its mother dead in a bog hole and lugged it in and everything. Bill did better, for after he dragged the cow out and skinned her (I just couldn't have done that) Mr. R. said Bill could keep all he got for the hide. That was $2.00

3.20 . . This should be the total. But I've really got only $2.70 unless Bill pays back $.50 which I had to lend him. He sold chewing gum like I did blueing. He was awfully popular in school while he had the gum. But Bill shouldn't have passed it 'round. Was he scared when the company

> kept writing for the money. Daddy told him he must get it. He did, too, all but $.50. He squared that with the company by telling them to keep the skates he was to get for a premium."

To Mary's relief and joy, Don was sober-faced as he returned the note book after reading this last entry. She explained, "Bill's holding out on me. He got that two dollars this spring and some more for muskrat pelts. . . . You remember the gum? It was last summer."

Don rumpled the back of his thick hair. "It's not enough, but maybe Mustang'll talk turkey if— You wouldn't want me to put up a couple of dollars—if I could?"

"You were thinking of that, Don? No-o. It wouldn't be—" Mary stopped, startled by a noise. It was Chet Reardon standing at the open door, a smug grin on his round face. Just behind him was his horse with a brand new saddle on its back. It was the squeaking of the new leather which Mary had heard.

"Hu-huh, Mary's got a feller! Mary's got a feller!" Chet jeered.

Anger bringing out bright red flags in her cheeks, she cried, "How long have you been there?"

"Now wouldn't you like to know! . . . Heck! If I wanted a horse, or anything, I'd just buy it."

Mary could have cheered as Don asked pointedly, "With your dad's money, Chet?" And Chet, who had never earned a dollar, all at once got even redder than Mary.

Fortunately, the clash was avoided when Bill's voice called, "Hi, Don, come and look at Chet's new hull.* It's a pippin!"

School went rather badly for all the girl scholars on this day. The boys didn't come around at recess or the noon hour to play "steal-sticks" or "ante-over." They were much more interested in Chet's new saddle, and Chet strutted and bragged. Then for some reason he got excused and rode away before school was out.

Mary resented this favoritism on teacher's part. But Chet often boasted, "My folks are so important no teacher'd dast to buck 'em." So he did just about as he pleased.

When school was dismissed, Mary hoped she'd get another word with Don. But he rode away at once, and even Bill's being very nice to her didn't help to cheer her. She knew Brother Bill so well!

As they rode home, he talked of everything except the "something" which had him all excited. He wasn't fooling Mary in the least and at last she asked, "What do you want from me this time, Bill?"

Bill looked around, the freckles standing out on his bright face. "Uh? Well, it's this way, Sis. Chet'll swap his old saddle for this old relic of mine and five dollars to boot. Now I've got two and a

---

* Means saddle

half, and I thought if you'd lend me the other two and a half—"

"Bill," she said earnestly, "if you'd pay what you owe me and lend me only one dollar and eighty cents, I could buy Torchy. Why not do something for me just this once?"

"Torchy?" Bill said. "Oh, Chet knows about that pony. That's why he left school early—to make a deal with Mustang."

Mary felt as if she'd been bruised and beaten. "All right, Bill, you win," she said in a tired, unhappy voice.

Later that night she cried into her pillow. Now that she had lost the chance to buy Torchy nothing mattered. Don Murphy didn't really like her. He'd let her talk to him only because he was polite. He didn't care whether or not she got a horse. No one cared.

On the following morning, which was Saturday, Bill was eager to be on his way to the Reardon ranch.

"I'm going too," Mary told him.

"Aw, my gosh!" Bill sputtered. "A fellow don't always want to be seen riding double with his kid Sis!"

Mary looked him straight in the eyes. "It's worse for me than for you," she choked. "But I'm going to see that you don't get cheated . . . Remember the chewing gum, Bill."

The chewing gum being a sore point, Bill flushed and mumbled grudgingly, "Okay then."

At the Reardon ranch Mary was surprised to

see Don Murphy with Chet in front of the big red-roofed stable. Tied to the corral fence was Don's saddler and the trimmest coal black pony Mary had ever seen!

"That must be Torchy," she thought. And the desire to own the pony was all at once like—like a fire burning inside her.

Don had touched his dusty slouch hat to the girl. Chet, however, completely ignored the newcomers. Mary heard him saying:

"Sure glad you brought the cayuse to me, Don. Mustang said he was out on the range with a bunch and he'd have to corral 'em, else I'd have brought Torchy home myself."

Mary felt her cheeks burn. Was this "deal" spite work on Chet's part because she had often snubbed the one boy in school who boasted he could get anything he wanted? She'd been taught not to have mean thoughts of anyone, but couldn't she be excused this once? If only there was some way of taking Chet down a few pegs!

Don leaned easily against the corral fence, saying no word while Chet and Bill made their saddle trade. Chet thrust the "boot" money carelessly into his pocket and Bill cinched the much-wanted saddle on old Pete.

"Boy!" enthused Bill. "Is it a honey!"

"It's nice he's happy," thought Mary. "I should be lots gladder than I am that one of us is happy."

Don flicked a glance toward her. In his eyes was a noticeable twinkle which she did not understand. He asked, "You'll want to try out Torchy, Chet?"

"What do you think I am, a green horn?" demanded Chet. "Any smart trader always tries out a horse before he closes a deal."

Don held the pony while Chet put his new saddle on its short, round back. Torchy laid back one ear and cocked a suspicious eye at the saddle. The new leather squeaked every time he took a breath. Squeak! Squeak! Squeak!

Handing Torchy's reins to Chet, Don quickly swung to the back of his own buckskin. Again he glanced at Mary with the mischief in his dark eyes more evident than before.

Chet had lifted himself to his new saddle. It squeaked louder than ever, and Torchy suddenly went crazy. His wild snort could have been heard for a mile. He ducked his head low to the ground, bounded high into the air and landed pitching.

Mary would never forget the stunned expression on Chet's smug face when, bounced and shaken, he lost both stirrups. Then he somersaulted over Torchy's head and hit the hard ground. Thud!

Spurring his buckskin forward, Don caught Torchy's bridle reins, halted the pony, and took off the saddle at once. Bill, who liked Chet no better than his sister, exploded a laugh. "Reached for the horn and grabbed a handful of dirt!" he whooped.

Mary wanted to cheer, too. Watching Chet pick himself up, she was somehow reminded of a soap bubble pricked by a pin.

"So," said Chet and he glanced at Don, "you

tried to sell me a man-killing outlaw! I'm wise now. The deal's off!"

"The deal's off," Mary cried under her breath. "Then I can buy— Oh! I haven't any money."

"Outlaw?" Don drawled. "Shucks, Mary can ride this pony bareback."

"Mary ride that bronc *bareback?* You're crazy."

Don's eyes were twinkling again. "Chet, if you're game to put up five dollars to see Torchy ridden, Mary'll ride him."

"If he bucks I can't do it," thought Mary, half frightened. "But I'll try! . . . What's Don up to?"

Chet shouted, "I'll be tickled pink to put up the five spot. I won't lose the money and I'll have a picnic seeing Mary Phillips take an awful spill!"

Mary was now thrilled and excited. It was wonderful to have Don boosting for her. It was even more wonderful to have him help her to Torchy's round back and hand her the bridle reins.

She rode the pony around in short circles at a walk, at a trot, and at a lope. He was nervous and a bit skittish, but he didn't try to buck or object to his new rider.

Acting for Mary, Don took the five dollars from crestfallen, sullen Chet Reardon who complained, "I've been whipsawed somehow."

This complaint was the only thing which bothered Mary as, still riding Torchy, she and Don and Bill took the road for home. She waited until Bill had loped ahead before she asked, "Don, you didn't really trick Chet, did you? I mean do something to make Torchy buck?"

Don chuckled. "No trick. 'Twas Chet's brand new saddle. Torchy'd never had a squeaky thing like that on his back. So I'd guessed what would happen. And I've got *your* five dollars to give Mustang. That's half the price for Torchy, and he's now your pony! That make everything all right, Mary?"

"Everything is all right, Don!" Mary almost sang the words. She smoothed Torchy's mane, then looked up at the dark boy who rode so easily beside her and saw him smiling at her.

Ride 'Im Chick Norris!

JOSEPH S. FLEMING
(Powder River Joe)

A WILD bronc plunged out of the saddling chute; a twisting, pitching, wall-eyed bay. A tall young rider was riding the "hurricane deck" bending to the whip of the bucking outlaw.

The crowd roared.

"Rid 'im, Chick Norris!"

The bay, lashed to a frenzy by his failure to unseat that unwelcome burden on his back, suddenly whirled against the corral fence with a terrific whip-like motion. Chick Norris felt his right leg go numb. A sickening sensation arose in the pit of his stomach. He struggled to keep that leg moving to the swing of the pitching bronce. He was off balance. He had a feeling of being lifted, going higher and higher as though an invisible hook had him by the scruff of the neck. A twisting plunge. He shot through the air and lit all in a heap.

Chick glimpsed two men running toward him through the haze of blurred eyes. They wouldn't carry *him* off! He got to his feet stiffly and limped away just as two mounted cowpunchers roped the fiery bay, still plunging and kicking. Chick kept his eyes on the ground, busily dusting himself with his big hat—humiliated. Thrown—at Roaring Fork! A little two-by-four rodeo where he had won such a short time ago. And he—entered at Cheyenne—pitted against the best Top Hands in the whole country.

"This younger generation can't stand the gaff like the old timers," commented a leathery-faced old cattleman, making sure that the young rider could hear, though he was addressing his companions squatted along the fence rail. "Too soft—when things get soft they rot. And that's the young man of the twentieth century."

Chick stabbed the cattleman with a fiery glance. He was about to exclaim, "Well what do you expect with a bad leg if that cayuse—" but he swallowed his words. "No real Top Hand ever makes an alibi," he reminded himself. He glanced about the arena but all eyes were on another streak of bucking horse flesh. The show had gone on and he was forgotten.

Chick Norris rode along in gloomy silence as the Scouts of the Mounted Patrol jogged along over the mountain trail headed toward their camp on Roaring Fork. The annual two-weeks' encampment of these mounted Scouts of the range country had just received a jolt. How confident and light-hearted they had all ridden over to the Roaring Fork rodeo that morning. Their Patrol Leader, Chick Norris, was going to ride and sure would win. For hadn't he won at Roaring Fork at the last rodeo by conquering old Dynamite?

Ed Lake, Assistant Patrol Leader, straightened in his saddle as he glanced about at the downcast faces of his comrades.

This would never do. Imagine this happy, hard-riding bunch of Scouts sneaking back into camp like whipped coyotes!

"I'll be the first hombre into camp!" yelled the Assistant Patrol Leader as he whirled his cowpony off the trail and galloped across the meadow toward the little American Flag waving high on a barren pine trunk. A shrill piercing cowboy "Yi-i-i-ip!" in unison and the canyon walls, already darkened by the approaching twilight, resounded with the thundering hooves of the galloping cowponies.

The bean hole was quicky uncovered and the hungry lads sat down to a meal of steaming hot beans well seasoned with molasses. Then to top it all off, the grinning Shorty, who had remained behind to guard camp, presented six nicely browned rainbow trout.

Around the little camp fire that night, jokes and sharp shafts of wit shot back and forth as Ed Lake led in the determined endeavor to revive Chick's spirits. The light-hearted atmosphere penetrated the gloom of the Patrol Leader and he joined in the hearty laughter.

Yet, underneath, every Scout knew there was bitter disappointment. Although proud of the fact that their Patrol was led by Chick Norris, they would not be satisfied until their leader had reached that coveted goal of every cowpuncher—bronc-riding champ. As the Patrol Leader arose and walked from the circle of firelight, every eye followed the fading shadow of that tall, straight, muscular form walking along the trail with the roll of the horseman who has spent his life in the saddle. He was headed for a "final look at the horses." But the scouts knew there was another reason. He wanted to be alone while he battled those sharp shafts of disappointment within.

It was late that night when Ed Lake carefully unrolled the secret code of the Mounted Patrol and read it slowly and impressively while the Scouts stood at attention about the dying embers of the camp fire and raised their gauntlet gloved hands in solemn pledge as the words came from Ed's lips:

"On my honor, I will as a rider of the Mounted Patrol:
Ride hard.
Do the small things I don't want to do.
Shoot square.
Stick by my word.
Keep always on the watch.
Always come back with the stock.
Never go back on a friend."

When Chick Norris rode into the Diamond Bar corral on Sandy, leading his pack horse, Bat Martin was there to meet him.

"Wal, kid, I hear yuh got thrown at Roarin' Fork," Bat was calmly coiling a rope.

"Yea—by a bay," Chick loosened the perfect diamond on the pack horse. "Rocking Chair—cracked my leg against the corral fence if—"

"Kin yuh take it?"

Chick whirled. He looked into the cowpuncher's blazing eyes. Never had Bat spoken like that to him before. Then he understood. A whine had crept into his voice and he knew Bat could forgive a man anything but a whine. He threw back his shoulders—they had been drooping—he had not shown up so well in defeat. He looked the cowpuncher straight in the eye.

"Sure, I can take it."

Bat's piercing eyes softened and he continued slowly coiling his rope.

"Kid, you've been ridin' 'em high, wide an' handsome till yuh forked a fence peeler. An' he got yuh. You've got to ride fence peelers too, yuh know. Take a little advice from an ole cowpuncher—and don't think I'm tryin' to preach—" he placed a muscular arm on the shoulder of the youth. "All through life yu've got to ride yore fence peelers along with the rest. Yuh can't always pick yore broncs. Yuh can't always have success. Yu'll be thrown many a time—but it's the hombre that gets right up an' forks 'em again that wins out. That's it—always comin' back."

"Dynamite went through the fence with me, you know."

"But a fence peeler works different. He side-swipes as he grazes the fence aimin' to knock yore leg loose so's he can send yuh a-kitin'. Now rub down Sandy and yore pack hoss and we'll have a lesson on fence peelin' broncs by Professor Bat Martin, Doctor o' cowboyology."

Bat's wide grin melted away all icy gloom, and the youth led his horses off to the stable—whistling.

The Mounted Patrol jogged into Cheyenne; a riot of color, flags, bright-colored neckerchiefs, "ten-gallon" hats—the year before they had been five-gallon caliber—and a happy jostling throng of tourists, cowpunchers, cowgirls and townspeople. Frontier Days!

Chick rode over to the big tent. He thrilled as he jostled among the husky bronzed Top Hands of the range. At last he had won the right to battle in the lists with these knights of the stirrup. He reached into the big hat held high by the chief judge and drew out a slip of paper. "TNT," he read.

"What did yo' all get?" asked a big rawboned Texan at his elbow.

"TNT."

"Wal, kid, he ain't so bad. I drew him last year and he only gave me two busted ribs."

Bronc after bronc plunged, twisted and pitched across the big arena. Some riders stuck to the accompanying roar of the stands. Others were whirled off into the dust to accompanying groans.

"Chick Norris, of the Diamond Bar, out of chute number seven, on 'TNT'!" came through the horns over the judges' stand.

Chick, grim, every muscle tense, raised his right hand as he sat on the quivering horse. The gate swung wide. "TNT" plunged straight ahead, then took to swapping ends. Chick caught the swing of the pitching and swung his legs in perfect rhythm. He finished his ride without breaking a rule, and he knew he had been placed in the first division.

"Nice goin', kid."

Chick flushed at the ring of cheers, then checked his elation. "Don't get too cocky, Chick Norris. There's tough ridin' ahead!" he cautioned his inner self.

Bat Martin delivered a beautiful ride on Cart Wheel, Curly Johnson made a perfect score on a fighting roan and the Diamond Bar had placed men in the first division. The Diamond Bar cowpunchers were elated.

"Boy, howdy!" exclaimed Catfish Saunders, hitting his leather chaps a resounding slap with his big hat. "We're sure to cop the bronc-bustin' honors at this man's rodeo. And the way this Kid Norris is comin' along. If he can only stand the gaff—yuh know these young kids don't seem to have the stuff the old cowpuncher's got—soft livin'."

Chick Norris, flushing from the praise, changed within to smoldering anger. "That same old line about the younger generation," he muttered savagely between clenched teeth. Well, he could show them that all the he-men weren't born in the nineteenth century.

The semi-finals.

The bronc-riding competition was narrowing down. Chick, Curly and Bat Martin were still in the running. The keenness of the contest had lashed every cowpuncher to a daredevil fury that kept the crowds constantly on edge. The broncs became wilder and wilder.

Chic drew Whirl Wind.

"Fence Peeler," commented Bat Martin dryly. His piercing eyes burned into those of the young Diamond Bar rider. Chick's jaw clenched as he gave a hitch to his chaps. He knew what lay behind Bat's eyes.

Whirl Wind tore out of the chute, diving, sideswiping, sunfishing in a mad bucking plunge.

Chick held a tight seat, swinging in rhythm with every pitch.

With a squeal of rage Whirl Wind suddenly wheeled and whipped against the corral fence. Chick felt a sickening blow upon his knee. The arena whirled drunkenly before him. Then his head cleared with a neck-jerking lunge that brought him to his senses.

"One, two, three, four, five," he mumbled between clenched teeth. He dare not miss a stroke with those swinging legs. Two riders galloped up on either side and Chick slipped off, putting his weight upon his sound left leg.

Ed Lake was right there with Sandy. Painfully,

trying his best to hide his injury, Chick climbed onto Sandy.

"Ed, send two Scouts to the camp. I've got to get hot towels on his knee right away."

Bat Martin's grinning, "Nice goin', Kid," drove all pain away for an instant.

Then, over the amplifier—

"Chick Norris of the Diamond Bar wins a place in the finals tomorrow."

Boy, howdy! He would ride with one leg if he had to.

Chick Norris lay on his blankets, knee swathed in steaming towels. Red and Shorty kept a supply constantly boiling over the camp fire.

Two riders approached.

"Ditch that bucket of towels," exclaimed Chick, rising and pulling down his overall leg. "It's Curly Jenkins and Catfish Saunders of the Diamond Bar."

From the grimness of the approaching riders Chick sensed that something was wrong.

"How do yuh feel, kid?" greeted Curly, swinging off at the camp fire.

"Oh, I'm all right. Just bruised my knee a little."

Curly looked doubtfully at the leg the lad was standing on rather lightly a moment, then shoved his big hat back.

"Wal, kid, yo're all that's left o' the Diamond Bar to ride in the finals tomorrow."

"How about you, Curly?"

"I didn't quite make it."

"And Bat Martin?"

"Bat made it but—they just wrangled him off

to the hospital with a sudden attack of appendicitis. Goin' to operate."

There was black agony in Curly's eyes and a deep gloom settled over the Scouts circled about.

Chick choked a moment—good old Bat Martin—controlled himself and said firmly, "I'll do my best, Curly."

"I know yuh will, kid. I was sittin' on that corral fence when ole Whirl Wind cracked yore knee against it and I could feel those big timbers shake. I was jest wonderin'—that's all. The judges have switched yuh to the mount that Bat drew for the finals, ole Firebrand. He's a bad hoss. But yuh can top 'im all right, an' make a perfect score."

"I'll be right there on the hurricane deck when the time comes," declared Chick. "And I'll give all I've got."

" 'Atta boy, Chick. . . . The ole pepper." Curly and Catfish both gave the young rider an encouraging slap on the shoulder, swung up and loped away.

Chick stared after the disappearing riders.

"Regular guys—but hang it all—don't they think this younger generation's got any stuff?"

"They'll change their minds tomorrow, old kid," declared Ed Lake. "Now, let's get at the knee again."

The Mounted Patrol rode over to the arena right after a light lunch.

Already, the gay crowd wearing bright-colored neckerchiefs and big hats was filing into the stands. In the corrals the Top Hands were working with the stock, fighting with tough outlaw broncs as they "wrangled" them into the bucking chutes. On the race track a hundred Scouts were building bridges, signaling with flags from high towers speedily erected, bandaging victims and pitching camp. The Mounted Patrol threw diamond hitches, staged mounted drills and performed trick-riding feats, winding up with a Mounted color guard ceremony that brought every one to his feet in respect to The Flag.

All these activities kept the early arrivals on edge while waiting for the main events.

Chick Norris rode Sandy restlessly about Frontier Park. Partly to keep his injured leg limbered to the curve of the horse and partly because he craved action.

He rode up to the outlaw corral and peered over the bars.

Over in one corner stood a wall-eyed bay, standing listlessly, yet with ears laid back in a manner that showed him ever ready for battle.

"Rocking Chair!" exclaimed Chick aloud.

The negro stable boy perched on the top rail near by snorted.

"Boy, he may be Rockin' Chair to yo' all, but he's de Debbel an' all de Debbel's hooves to yo'ahs truly."

"Who's going to ride him?"

"Nobuddy now. Cowpuncher by name o' Norris drew him yesterday. But when Bat Martin collapsized wid his 'pendicks dey all gabe Norris his bronc Firebran' to ride. Firebran's a tough one but he ain't no fence peeler like dat ole streak o' fire an' brimstone ober dar in de co'ner. Rockin' Chair! Har, har, har!"

Chick stared in deep thought at the bay. Then his face lit with the gleam of an idea that flashed across his mind. His drawn slip of paper had read "R.C." Rocking Chair, of course. He hadn't thought of that. Curly Jenkins knew though, and had told the Diamond Bar men the kid couldn't last out on this fence peeler. Then they had persuaded the judges to let him ride Firebrand. All in good faith of course, no contestant had objected. To the Diamond Bar men, winning the championship was the big thing—they didn't know about any other objective. A roar and a cloud of dust from the arena told him that the cowpunchers had gone into action. Too late now. His name would be called any minute—

A horseman suddenly whirled alongside, pulling up to a slithering stop.

It was Ed Lake reaching out a gauntleted hand which held an envelope.

Feverishly Chick tore it open and stared at the penciled scrawl:

"Ride 'im, Chick Norris—for me.
Bat Martin."

Chick swallowed hard.

The last thought of Bat as he had gone into another world under the influence of the anesthetic had been of the kid he taught cowpunching from the cradle up. And now, hovering between life and death, the satisfaction that Chick was out there riding his heart out was the best stimulant of all. As clear as if in that hospital room looking down at Bat, he could see a flash in the eyes, though weakened and he could hear Bat urge feebly, but emphatically:

"Ride that *fence peeler*. Ride 'im, Chick Norris!"

Chick jerked out a pencil and scrawled a note on the back of Bat's paper:

"Nurse—please read this telegram to Bat Martin. It'll be good medicine."

> "Good old Bat—I've picked Rocking Chair, that old fence peeler that got me at Roaring Fork—so help me hannah, I'm going to take that bronc for a ride.
>
> "Chick."

"Ed, get this telegram off to the hospital right away. I've got to ramble along."

Ed Lake stared in amazement after the young cowpuncher galloping like mad toward the arena, read the telegram, smiled knowingly, and galloped into action.

The amplifiers had stopped—the crowd leaned forward anticipating an important announcement.

"L-a-dies and g-e-ntlemen! There is a change on the program. Chick Norris of the Diamond Bar will endeavor to ride Rocking Chair instead of

Firebrand from choice. This hard-ridin' kid has an old score to settle with this man-killin' bronc. Out of chute number one."

A hush.

Everyone leaned forward.

In the chute the kid settled himself and grimly looked through the bars at the gate tender.

"Let 'er buck!"

The gate flew open. For a tense second horse and rider stood framed within the narrow pen. Chick leaned back, gripping tight with his legs, eyes riveted on that lantern-jawed head watching for the first jump. Suddenly, with a squeal of rage, Rocking Chair leaped into the open. He stopped. Shook his head. Chick reached forward with his wrapped spur rowels and raked the bronc from shoulder to thigh. The bay stood up—up, he was going over backward! Chick loosened himself. No. The bay suddenly changed his plans. He whirled, pivoted on his heels, gave a long twisting jump and leaped at the big plank gate on chute number four.

"Fence Peeler! . . . Look out . . ."

Chick swung in his right heel with a vicious jab, putting all power he had in that injured leg and fairly lifted the man killer around. The bronc threw in a snaky side-swiping twist and grazed the big post as he went by, sweeping the rider's leg back. A groan from the stands, Chick reeled an instant as his leg went numb, sharp shooting pains penetrating his whole body. Then with a savageness that drove out all thought of injury, he roused himself and swung his legs fore and aft, sticking tight to the saddle. The plunging, wall-eyed bay got the backwash of the feeling he had aroused in that young rider. The roar of the stands filled the arena. Revolt raced through Chick's mind. Bend to the whip of the horse. Fence peeler, eh? The kid can't take it, yuh say! Well, old Rocking Chair, Chick Norris is ridin' fence peelers these days. He fanned the bronc with his big hat at every jump. Back and forth zigzagged the furious bay, aviating, sunfishing —springing everything in the bronc's curriculum —but that wild man on his back was still in the saddle sticking like a leech. A pistol cracked. Chick felt himself going. The arm of the pickup man lifted him free—and the roaring arena went spinning from him.

The clank, clanking of spurs resounded through the hushed silence of the hospital corridor.

A somewhat paled, bronzed face, framed in a white pillow, lit up with a grin.

"It's them kids, nurse. Let 'em in."

The nurse smiled her greeting in the hallway.

"Come right in, boys. You have been a great tonic to Mr. Martin."

Chick Norris limped into the room followed by his leathery young comrades.

"Wal, Scouts, they've got me throwed and tied, but not for keeps."

A grin spread around the circle of youthful, bronzed faces. That was Bat Martin for you. Never downed. Always fighting.

"Chick, that was a great ride. The signal men of the Mounted Patrol hooked me up to the arena and I followed every move. Boy, it was great medicine. In the eyes o' the judges yuh lost the championship on technical points—but yuh conquered that fence peeler and in the eyes o' old Bat Martin, that's bein' champ. An' only you and I know what that means. I want to shake the hand o' the gamest kid that ever forked a bronc."

The Mounted Patrol cantered briskly out of Cheyenne and headed toward the purple hills that held the home range land.

Chick Norris, on Sandy, rode in the lead—head up and whistling.

Ba-ee

KATHRYN COOK

IT WAS late afternoon when Johnnie Blue Feather stopped to rest on a low, flat rock beside the trail to the cliffs. The way was difficult for him because of his crippled foot. It dragged along behind him, weak and clumsy, and the stones in the path were sharp against his flesh.

Johnnie hated his foot. All his life he had ached to run and play with the other boys of the tribe, but his foot mocked him. It spoiled everything, even the Fourth of July celebrations.

Only yesterday, Johnnie and his family had returned to the reservation after spending three days near the fairgrounds with the other Arapaho Indians. For three days he had yearned over the gay, swift ponies other boys rode in the races, while his heart grew bitter with longing.

Astride a pony, Johnnie would have been strong and swift also. People wouldn't know then that he couldn't walk like the rest, and they would stop pitying him. But Gregory Blue Feather, Johnnie's father, could ill afford even the ancient team of horses that pulled the family wagon. He had all he could do to feed his eight children.

Johnnie was a handsome lad, and sturdy too, except for his foot. His hair was thick and black, and lay smooth as heavy silk down the back of his neck. His arms and shoulders were firm and brown, with muscles that rippled beneath his faded blue shirt. There was no finer lad in all the tribe, had it not been for his limp. With a pony to ride, he would have been as any other boy.

Johnnie glanced down again at the camp. The Little Wind River stretched away across the reservation, a thin ribbon of green winding its way through dull gray.

The boy scowled at them. He sent one last rock hurtling down and continued his climb, brooding over the past three days in town. In the winter, at Government school, he scarcely noticed his infirmity, for his brain was nimble, if his body was not; but in the summer, with races, and hunts, and celebrations, life seemed very difficult indeed.

So wrapped up in misery was the boy that he almost stumbled over the dead mare before he saw her. Flies were beginning to crawl in and out of the nostrils, and on the air hung the odor of death.

Johnnie recoiled. Then he saw the newborn colt. It was standing on uncertain legs beside a rock a few feet away. The boy's eyes lost their glaze of apathy. They widened in surprise. The colt was beautiful, standing there against the dull gray of the boulder.

Johnnie's heart pounded hard against his ribs. He longed to rush forward and touch the colt, but he hesitated. He must not frighten it. Instead, he reached into his trouser pocket for a piece of cooky. It was crumpled and moist, and as he drew it out, a raisin or two dropped to the ground.

"Here, Ba-ee," he called softly to the colt, so shiny-red in the afternoon sun that it reminded him at once of a new copper penny. "Come, Ba-ee, come, little penny."

The baby drew back its ears and snorted with fright. It tried to jump away, but the spindly legs collapsed. It sprawled grotesquely on the ground, letting out a surprised, stricken sound.

Johnnie dropped to his knees and crooned to the frightened animal. "Don't be afraid, little red one," he said. "Can't you see I'm your friend?"

He edged closer to the fallen colt, speaking softly as he moved, and holding the cooky crumbs before him. His heart thumped with longing and joy as the space between him and the colt became smaller, smaller, until finally he was gazing right into the deep violet eyes of the animal, eyes that were wide with fear.

He crouched motionless for a moment, making soft noises in his throat. The colt nickered and tried to get up. Johnnie reached out and put one arm gently beneath the thin body. Suddenly, miraculously, the baby was on its legs again, but this time it stood still, flanks quivering with the effort, ears moving back and forth, experimentally.

For several seconds the two of them, the wonder-struck boy and the newborn colt, stood side by side. Then the colt thrust its moist nose inquiringly into Johnnie's middle with a nudging motion.

"Why, you are hungry!" the boy exclaimed, and unclenched his fist.

But Ba-ee wasn't interested in crumbs and raisins. He made small disappointed noises and nudged Johnnie again, this time more insistently.

"It's milk you want, isn't it, little cayuse?" the boy said, tossing the crumbs aside.

The colt prodded him again. The violet eyes were soft and pleading now. Johnnie glanced around. No other animal was to be seen. The mare must have belonged with a band of wild horses that roamed the plains beyond camp.

A thought struck Johnnie. The colt was an orphan! It had no owner. Could he not, then, claim it for his own?

His heart thumped wildly. He put out an eager hand. The skin on the colt's back quivered briefly beneath his touch and was still. The short, bristly red hair felt warm and alive. He stroked the thin flank lovingly while Ba-ee stood motionless in the warm afternoon sunshine, his legs stiff and uncertain, his short mop of a tail dangling foolishly.

"Ba-ee, my every own," Johnnie said, testing the words. They sounded sweet to his ears, very sweet. "But how can I feed you?" he asked, his eyes dark with concern.

He thought of the rough trail that led down to camp. Ba-ee was too weak to make the trip, he knew. Besides that, Johnnie was sure that the moment his brothers set eyes on the colt, it would no longer belong to him. Had they not always taken everything from him?

He looked about him. They were in a sort of arena, surrounded on three sides by sandstone boulders. The other side sloped away into the open prairie. There was no water up here, and very little grass. Unless he could bring food to him, Ba-ee would soon starve to death.

Suddenly he remembered old One Horn, the brindled cow that supplied milk for the morning oatmeal. If he could lead her up here, after dark, she might have enough milk left to feed Ba-ee.

Johnnie's spine tingled. It was a small chance, but it might work out. It had to! Ba-ee must have food, and soon. With all he had ever prayed for so near at hand, Johnnie dared not fail.

He gazed impatiently at the sky. It would be hours before he could bring One Horn up here. What if the colt died of hunger in the meantime? His own stomach told him it was almost time for the evening meal.

He gave Ba-ee one last pat and turned to go. The animal nickered piteously. Johnnie turned back, his throat tight. "Don't you worry, little cayuse," he said thickly. "I'll come back to you. Please wait for me."

He stumbled hastily down the path, his heart

straining to stay with the small hungry creature in the boulders.

It seemed to Johnnie that time stood still between supper and bedtime. He found it almost impossible to sit quietly beside the campfire while the boys made plans for the hunt. Then he tossed and turned in the darkness of the tepee, waiting for his brothers to drop off to sleep so that he could steal away. Finally, when all had been quiet for moments, Johnnie screwed up courage to slip out. There was only a faint sliver of a moon in the sky. He stood quietly for a time, and then headed for the river, dragging his foot slowly so the dogs would not be disturbed.

"Whoo!" came a cry close by, and the boy's heart lurched sharply before he realized it was only an owl. He noticed the familiar cow smell on the night air and knew One Horn was near. He stopped to listen. The slow, even chewing sound told him where to go.

"So, Bossie, so, Bossie," he whispered as he found the end of her tether and loosened it. He gave a gentle tug. One Horn lowed, and Johnnie tensed and held his breath, praying that no one had been awakened. The camp was quiet. The outlines of the tepees stood out white against the dark sky. Johnnie tugged at the rope again. This time the cow responded and soon they were circling the camp, headed for the cliffs.

Suddenly the boy stiffened and dropped to the ground silently. Footsteps came to him on the quiet air. Someone was coming down the path a few feet away! He scuttled into the sagebrush, dropping the end of the rope in his rush. His heart stopped beating as the steps drew nearer, paused, and then continued on in the direction of camp. He squatted there for an eternity, until he could no longer distinguish the footsteps from the sound of the cow's jaws, munching.

When he got up and groped around for the tether, his knees felt strange. It had been a close call. Slowly they made their way upward again. It seemed to the boy that the journey was unending. The rocks looked different in the dark too—large, and unfriendly. He began to worry lest he miss Ba-ee.

One Horn pulled back stubbornly a time or two, impatient with this strange mission, but finally they reached the arena. The bulk of the dead mare appeared. Johnnie looked around for the colt, but all he could see were twisted rocks, strange in the moonlight.

He swallowed a sudden panic. What if Ba-ee had strayed into the open prairie? He would never find him in the darkness! He made a large circle, but the colt was nowhere to be seen.

"He's gone!" Johnnie said aloud, and his voice quavered. There was a moment's silence, and then a small sound came to him. He stopped short. There it was again, from the direction of the dead horse! In a rush he was beside the carcass. There in the dim light he saw Ba-ee, curled up in the shelter of his dead mother's body, as though seeking warmth and protection! The colt whinnied feebly. Johnnie let out a cry of relief.

"You d-d-d-did wait," he stuttered. "You did wait, after all!"

He rushed to the cow and tugged impatiently on the rope. "Hurry, hurry," he urged, but smelling the dead horse, One Horn braced her forefeet and refused to budge one inch closer. Johnnie pulled and threatened and poked, but she was immovable. Nor could he bring the colt to her. It was too weak to rise.

He sat down on a boulder to plan. With victory so near, there must be some way!

Suddenly an inspiration came to him. He pulled out his red bandanna handkerchief and went over to the cow. After several tugs, a thin stream of milk sprayed forth. He squeezed again and again until the handkerchief was dripping with the warm, pungent stuff. Then he ran to Ba-ee and thrust it beneath the colt's nose.

"Food, little cayuse," he said eagerly.

Ba-ee sniffed and made a hungry sound. Then he nibbled daintily at one corner of the material. Johnnie held his breath. Ba-ee flung his head away, protesting. In desperation, the boy squeezed the wet cloth, catching the milk in his fist as it fell. He thrust it under the colt's nose. This time Ba-ee seemed to understand, for he put his velvety muzzle into Johnnie's palm. When he drew it away, his face was wet. He whinnied eagerly and tried to rise.

"No, no, you wait there," the boy said, scurrying back to the cow.

Many trips he made, until Ba-ee would take no more milk. He stopped to rest, excitement running high within him. He had won! He had found a way to feed his pet!

A fresh night wind ruffled the bushes and Johnnie shivered. He looked at Ba-ee lying there by his mother's cold body. He would soon be chilled too.

"I'll stay with you," the boy decided, not daring to think what would happen if they missed him down in camp.

He twisted the cow's tether about a bush and stretched out beside Ba-ee, pillowing his head on the thin ribs. The colt sighed deeply and then dropped off to sleep. Johnnie could feel the even rise and fall of the animal's ribs as he breathed, and a thrill of joy went through him.

He lay for what seemed hours, his mind alert with plans, his body tingling with the nearness of Ba-ee. He forgot that he was weak and clumsy, a despised cripple. Ba-ee was weak also, and he needed Johnnie's help. Someday, when Ba-ee had grown into a fine horse he would, in turn, serve his master, but for now, the boy was content to dream. One day Ba-ee would win the Fourth-of-July races; it made a fine dream, a very fine dream, indeed!

Johnnie awoke shivering in the gray dawn. He rubbed his eyes in confusion. Then his glance fell on Ba-ee, and he remembered. He rushed over to One Horn. She had plenty of milk for Ba-ee now.

The colt whinnied and struggled to its feet. Johnnie was overwhelmed with joy. Then Ba-ee came over to the cow. The boy sprayed milk at his pet until Ba-ee, exploring, found the source. One Horn looked back and shook her head once, and then returned to her grazing. Ba-ee's tail shivered in delight as he ate breakfast. He had found a new mother.

When he had finished eating, though, another problem arose. He didn't want to stay here alone while Johnnie and the cow returned to camp! Three times the boy chased him back and three times the colt trailed. Finally in desperation Johnnie tied the cow's rope loosely about Ba-ee's neck. He would, in time, work it off, but by then they would be down the trail and out of sight.

"There, you've got to stay put," he said, winding the end about a sagebrush.

The sky was beginning to turn pink. Before long the sun would appear. Johnnie threw his arms about Ba-ee's thin neck for a last hug. "Stay here like a good cayuse," he said, and rushed down the trail, One Horn ahead of him, racing the daybreak.

He was chilled when he crept into bed alongside his brothers. Luckily, it was still an hour or so before the camp would stir. He had left the cow down by the river, close to her feeding ground of last night. He lay sleepless in the quiet tepee, waiting for his family to waken, and wondering if Ba-ee had managed to worm his way out of the loose rope halter by now. If he hadn't, he might become tangled with a sagebrush and choke. A thousand fears rose before Johnnie as he lay there. Would day never come? Already he was straining to be back with his pet.

Finally he heard his mother stirring the iron kettle that held the oatmeal gruel. Then his father returned from milking, complaining that One Horn had lost her rope during the night and had gone roaming. There was little milk for breakfast, he told the children as he wakened them. Johnnie felt slight qualms of conscience, hearing this. Then he thought of the thinness of Ba-ee's sides, and how happy he had been with the milk, and resolved to pour no milk on his mush. His pet could have his share.

It was after breakfast that the blow fell upon Johnnie. He was making ready to steal away to the cliffs when his father spoke. "Johnnie, it is time you do something to earn your bread and meat," he said. "Your brothers are hunting rabbits for the soup pot today. You will help the squaws in the garden."

Johnnie grew pale at these words. How could he feed Ba-ee and work in the garden? The colt would die of thirst, or choke on the rope, or wander away into the prairie by nightfall! Still, there was nothing he could do. His father had spoken. He could not protest without betraying his secret.

He headed for the tribal garden, dragging his crippled foot through the dust listlessly, paying no attention to the taunts of his brothers. Little did they care that he must work with the squaws! They were strong and swift, and pulling weeds was already far beneath their dignity. They would hunt meat while Johnnie nursed vegetables.

He took his place among the women sullenly. His spirits were bruised, trampled in the dust. Gone were his fine dreams of last night when he had slept under the stars with Ba-ee. Today, Ba-ee would starve, while he, Johnnie, hoed in the garden!

The sun was well up in the heavens, and Johnnie's back had begun to ache from the unaccustomed work, when suddenly from the direction of the cliffs came excited whoops from his three brothers. Johnnie glanced up grimly, expecting to see that they were already returning to camp with many rabbits. What he saw made him jerk erect.

Even at that distance, he could recognize Ba-ee, moving along on uncertain legs, while his brothers prodded him with a stick. A cry of horror escaped his lips. No! No! They couldn't have found his pet so quickly! What could he do now?

He watched numbly while the triumphant group drew nearer and nearer to his father's tepee. A group of neighbors had gathered curiously there beside his mother and Pogy, waiting. If Johnnie was going to assert himself, now was the moment.

He put down his hoe carefully. With a heavy heart he left the garden and went toward the tepee.

His brothers were gesturing excitedly when he came up silently on the fringe of the crowd. Mink Tail was relating their discovery with great pride.

"And so we came upon him up on top, by the boulders, beside his dead mother. We can keep him, can't we, Father?"

The other boys broke in, chattering all at the same time, while Johnnie stood silently, his heart cold within him. Ba-ee was quivering, his eyes wild and afraid. The sight tore Johnnie's heart.

Gregory Blue Feather spoke to his sons. "It is no use to talk of keeping the colt," he said, shrugging. "It cannot live without its mother. It will starve to death in three days. You will see. But keep it until then. It will make good coyote bait later."

"No! No!" The words left Johnnie's throat before he realized it. He flung himself on Ba-ee's rough red neck and buried his nose in the shaggy fur. "You can't make coyote bait of him. He's mine! I found him first. I won't give him up!"

His father spoke sharply, a frown creasing his forehead. "What foolishness is this, my son? Your brothers have brought home a stray colt, and now you raise a fuss and say he is yours. Have you not been hoeing in the garden as I ordered? How, then, could you find a pony?"

Before Johnnie could reply, his brothers set up a wild clamor. "Johnnie is an old woman," they jeered. "He can only hoe in the garden, and now he claims the pony. What would he do? Teach it to pull a plow?"

Johnnie stood in stony silence, unable to speak up before so many curious bystanders. It was as he had known it would be. Once more his brothers had triumphed over him.

He turned away from the group and sought the river's edge. Sorrowfully he watched the waters swirl around the willows that fringed the bank. Ba-ee was lost to him. Once again the world was a dreary place.

He did not hear his mother until she stood beside him, until her soft voice sounded almost as low as the ripple of the water. "Tell me, Johnnie," she said, and her eyes were troubled. "Tell me about the pony you claimed as yours."

Johnnie gazed out across the water bleakly. "It is of no use, Mother," he said and sighed. "It is only that I dreamed, for a time, that at last I had found something to make up for—" he paused and glanced down at his foot—"for this." He was silent a moment. Then his shoulders straightened and he shrugged carelessly. "But it doesn't matter—not really. Father says the colt will—will starve anyhow. I should have known better than to dream such foolish dreams."

"Perhaps we could try to feed the little one," his mother said quietly. "We need not tell the others. It will be our secret."

A faint hope fluttered inside Johnnie. "You mean take milk from One Horn for him? Oh Mother, he can have my share! I won't miss it at all! Do you think that will be enough?"

His mother smiled faintly at his sudden spirit. "I think we can spare enough for the baby," she said. "Come, son, your father will be angry with you if you do not return to your hoeing."

The boy trudged back to the vegetables reluctantly. His heart was lighter than it had been, but although his mother had promised to feed Ba-ee, the colt was not his. He could hear the boys playing with the animal, and it seemed to him they were laughing loudly in order to tantalize him.

When darkness came and the family gathered around the campfire to eat the thick, pungent rabbit stew his mother had prepared in the iron kettle, Johnnie found his throat closing against food. Ba-ee lay beside a sagebrush, rousing now and then to nicker softly. The animal was hungry, but no one made the slightest move toward feeding it. Johnnie crouched as near him as he dared, lonely and miserable, wondering when his mother would in some way manage to bring Ba-ee milk.

When supper was finished and the other boys dashed off to play, Johnnie went over to Ba-ee and put out a longing hand. Ba-ee raised his head and nuzzled him. "No, little cayuse," the boy said brokenly, "I haven't anything to feed you. I haven't even the right to pet you now."

Alice Laughing Fawn found her son curled up beside the colt later when she came with a pan of milk. Both of them were dozing, and she stood silently a moment, looking down at the pair. Johnnie had one arm thrown over Ba-ee, protecting him, and his arm rose and fell lightly with the animal's breathing.

"He is good," she whispered into the night. "The Father gave me this crippled one only for comfort."

She stooped to waken Johnnie. He sprang up instantly. "You did bring food, after all," he said gladly. "Here, Ba-ee, see what we have for you!"

For three days the two of them fed Ba-ee whenever they could manage but the colt, instead of thriving, seemed to grow weaker and weaker, until one morning when Johnnie's brothers tried to pull him to his feet he refused. Finally Joe, annoyed, gave him one last prod with his moccasin and sniffed in disgust. "He's no good. We don't want him. Father can make coyote bait out of him whenever he wants."

Johnnie saw red flashes of fire around him. "Stop it!" he cried. "You leave Ba-ee alone! He's sick, can't you see?"

The boys laughed. "Look at Johnnie. What a big fuss he makes over that half-dead cayuse. Why don't you ride him, Johnnie?"

Alice Laughing Fawn had come to the door of the tepee to listen. "You bad, bad boys," she scolded, "leave Johnnie alone! He shall have the colt now. You have abused it long enough. Go find yourselves some other mischief! Away, all of you," she said, flourishing the wooden spoon she held.

The boys retreated. When they had gone Johnnie knelt down beside Ba-ee and cradled his head in hs lap. Ba-ee belonged to him, now, but he was dying. He touched the soft end of the colt's nose.

"Poor little Ba-ee," he said, trying to keep his voice steady. "Do not be afraid. I will watch over you, my little friend. I will not let them feed you to the coyotes, ever. Sleep, little cayuse, sleep."

All that day he stayed near, pleading with Ba-ee to sip small amounts of milk, but the colt grew steadily worse. The afternoon sun became unbearable, and Ba-ee's eyes glazed in the heat.

Gregory Blue Feather passed by and stopped to inspect the animal. "By tomorrow he will be dead," he observed. "A colt needs much rich, sweet milk —mare's milk. You can't raise them without it."

As his father went away, the boy's mind echoed his words. Sweet, rich milk was what Ba-ee needed, only where could he get it? Suddenly he jumped up and went to where his mother was beading moccasins in the shade of a large cottonwood tree.

"Mother, it is sugar Ba-ee needs," he said, his voice sounding out shrilly in the lazy afternoon. "Please, can I try some sugar in his milk?"

Alice Laughing Fawn paused in her work. "Sugar, my son?" she said, puzzled. "What makes you think that would help?"

"Father just said mare's milk is sweet and rich," Johnnie said urgently. "Please, Mother, let me try it! If we don't do something quickly, Ba-ee is going to—to—" his voice thickened and a huge lump rose in his throat.

His mother lay aside the moccasins and rose. "Come," she said, smiling gently, "we shall see if sugar will save Ba-ee. But don't count on it too much, my son. He is very weak by now."

She warmed milk and stirred a spoonful of sugar into it, and the two of them went to the colt. When she saw how he panted in the sun she shook her head. "You should find something to make a shelter for him, son. Go find a piece of old blanket.

We can drive stakes into the ground to hold it above him."

When Johnnie returned, his mother's face was pleased. "I believe he liked the milk, son. He drank most of it without my coaxing. We will give him more later. Here," she said, motioning, "plant the sticks firmly so the wind will not tear the blanket down."

In the comfort of the makeshift shelter, Ba-ee lay motionless. Johnnie hung over his pet, watching anxiously for any sign of improvement. Toward evening, Ba-ee raised his head. The boy was overcome with joy. He rushed to bring some more sweetened milk, and after Ba-ee had drunk it, the colt dropped off into a deep slumber.

Johnnie stretched out on the ground beside him, brushing away the mosquitoes and deer flies with an old sagehen wing. He lay quietly, listening to each breath Ba-ee took, almost afraid to move lest he disturb his pet.

After supper the other boys came by to inspect the colt curiously. Johnnie tensed, but they only stayed a moment. They were no longer interested in poor Ba-ee.

Laughing Fawn brought food to her son and watched while he ate it greedily. It was the first he had taken all day, for several days actually, except for listless picking.

She put a hand on his shoulder caressingly. "I think that perhaps you and Ba-ee will both live," she said softly, "now that you are together once more. But take care, my son, lest you love the colt too much."

As the squash and corn flourished in the summer, so Ba-ee also thrived, once he started on the road to recovery. The boy and his pet were seldom apart. If Johnnie weeded in the garden, the colt tagged along, nibbling at the clover that fringed the banks of the irrigation ditches. His coat gleamed like molten copper in the sun and his tail flirted impishly with the passing breezes.

Even Gregory Blue Feather had to admit at length that there was small chance of Ba-ee's becoming coyote bait. Johnnie's brothers said little, but he knew by their envious glances that they were regretting their desertion of the dying animal.

Possession gave Johnnie new courage. He no longer dreaded people, for now their eyes mirrored respect. Ba-ee was a camp favorite, and Johnnie's heart expanded with pride when people admired his pet.

They roamed the foothills together, the boy with one arm thrown over the husky shoulders of the colt for support as he dragged his crippled foot through the brush and rocks. He talked intimately with Ba-ee as they moved along—frivolous dreams that were growing within him, about the days when Ba-ee would become a famous race horse—the days when Ba-ee would win the Fourth-of-July races.

He watched with excitement as the colt's slim legs became strong and swift, and firm muscles rippled beneath the glossy hide. He longed to leap on the colt's back and race madly over the prairie. Instead, he lifted baby Pogy up and led Ba-ee sedately around the tepee while his little brother squealed in delight. There would be time enough for racing later, when Ba-ee was grown.

When the icy winds swept down from the north and turned the prairie into a sea of glistening white, Ba-ee became a teddy bear overnight. His coat was thick and bushy, and his slender legs looked short and stocky. It kept Johnnie scurrying to find enough for his pet to eat, for now he must go to school every day. It had been hard to bid Ba-ee good-by each morning, but the colt soon learned to wait in the lane for his master in the evening.

As winter wore on, and the supply of feed for Ba-ee became slim and finally vanished altogether, Johnnie became greatly concerned. Clearly, Ba-ee could not live on snow and straw alone. Already his sides were beginning to bulge dangerously from such a diet. All day he stood listlessly in the shelter of the strawstack, shivering. He no longer came to meet Johnnie in the lane at night. His eyes took on the old, pleading look the boy remembered so well. Ba-ee was hungry.

When Johnnie spoke to his father about it, Gregory Blue Feather shrugged impatiently. "We don't have enough salt pork and corn meal for ourselves. How could we feed a worthless cayuse?"

The boy knew his father spoke truly. Many a night, he went to bed with hunger pangs gnawing his middle. Baby Pogy's stomach looked round, like

Ba-ee's, from too many dried beans. It was a hard winter for them all.

The boy drooped over his mathematics, and grew dull in history. Finally, one of his teachers questioned him after class was dismissed.

"What troubles you, Johnnie?" she said, her kind face crinkling in concern. "All fall you were the brightest in your class, and now you become listless and faraway."

Johnnie shook his head without saying anything, his eyes glued on the floor. It would do no good to tell Miss Harper about Ba-ee. She was only a woman. She would not know what to do about a starving colt.

"How is your pony?" she asked suddenly.

Johnnie blinked. "You know Ba-ee?" he said in amazement.

The woman smiled, and a twinkle lighted her eyes. "And who doesn't?" she replied. "I love to walk in the lanes in the fall. I saw you and your pet many times. And how is he?" she persisted, watching his face closely.

Johnnie looked away. "He is hungry. I think perhaps he is starving." His voice was low.

"Oh?" Miss Harper's voice was low too, and ever so gentle. "And this troubles you, perhaps?"

Johnnie nodded mutely.

"Well, then, we must do something about it," the woman said. "How would you like to clean the schoolroom each night, Johnnie, in exchange for hay from the Government farm?"

For a moment the boy's mind could not grasp

the wonder of what she was offering. Then he smiled, and it was like the unfolding of a cactus blossom in the warm spring sun.

"Oh, yes, ma'am!" he cried. "Yes, that would be great! God bless you, ma'am!"

Working after school meant that Johnnie must trudge home in the dark instead of riding the school bus part way, but this was nothing to the boy. Ba-ee, fed with green, pungent alfalfa hay, became lively once more. Each night he awaited Johnnie's return eagerly, and the boy watched while his pet devoured the hay down to the last wisp.

Close upon the miracle of Ba-ee's salvation came the miracle of spring. By late April the prairies were dotted with wild paintbrush and shooting stars, and larkspur made whole hillsides bright blue.

Summer brought new problems, however. Overnight, Ba-ee became a horse. With his size, his popularity also grew, and it was all Johnnie could do to keep the boys of the tribe from stealing rides. He too wanted to ride, but he knew that if Ba-ee was to become a fine race horse, he must first grow strong and heavy. This was not the time to ride. Instead, he spent hours brushing Ba-ee's coat until it gleamed like satin. Then the two wandered along the river bottoms or through the sagebrush, content and lazy in the sun.

That summer, instead of spending his Fourth of July brooding over the dancers, Johnnie sought out a leather shop, and with his small savings he purchased buckles and a bit to use in fashioning

Ba-ee a fine bridle. Ba-ee must have the very finest bridle Johnnie could make. He would spend all winter working on it in the school workshop. It would have a beaded forehead piece, and smooth reins which he would fashion himself from leather his mother tanned. So busy was Johnnie that he almost forgot to brood over his foot. Next year he would show them. Next year he would show them all!

Winter found Ba-ee prepared this time. It was no longer necessary for Johnnie to forage for his pet. The yearling was sturdy and fat, and while he begged for the frequent offerings of hay from the Government stacks, he managed well enough without them.

Toward spring, Johnnie found his mind wandering from his lessons often. It was a difficult time. The lad knew that when the warm breezes had swept the snow from the land, Ba-ee would be ready to ride!

For two years he had dreamed of that time. Two years had changed both boy and horse. Johnnie was fifteen, almost a man, and the horse, slim and eager, waited like a red arrow poised in a bow.

It was a warm Saturday afternoon in late March when Johnnie led Ba-ee down the lane away from everyone so that the first mounting might be a private affair.

He found a smooth boulder from which he could reach the horse's back easily, and stood poised there a moment smoothing Ba-ee's silky mane.

Finally he threw his lame leg over the sleek red back.

A rider was not strange to Ba-ee, since he had carried Pogy all his life, but for Johnnie this was the supreme moment. The blood pounded in his temples. Beneath him he could feel life, Ba-ee's tense, waiting strength, like a million springs, all wound and eager for release.

He patted the curving neck and nudged Ba-ee's ribs gently. The horse moved forward in small, prancing steps, snorting in excitement. Johnnie could feel the muscles straining, and knew that if he made the sign, Ba-ee would be off across the prairie like a spurt of flame, racing the wind.

Instead, the boy spoke softly in Arapaho, and holding the reins firmly, he guided Ba-ee in large circles about the flat rock. For fifteen minutes they rode, round and round, until Johnnie felt the tide of excitement ebb away. Then he slipped from the moist red back. He must train Ba-ee gradually.

All that spring the two worked. Ba-ee learned to turn right or left with only a faint pressure of Johnnie's knee as a signal, and to start with the speed of an arrow. Happiness was like a warm cloud around Johnnie's heart. His crippled foot was of no concern to him now. He had four feet—four swift, polished hoofs beneath him, prancing and eager. Never again would he be lonely or sad. He had the dearest friend in all the world, Ba-ee.

Overnight it was July, and time for the celebrations. The evening before the tribe was to leave for Lander and the rodeo, Johnnie could not rest.

He crept out of the close air of the tepee and went to where Ba-ee was munching clover. He passed his hand over the glossy coat.

"Tomorrow we shall run in the race," he whispered into Ba-ee's twitching ear. "Tomorrow we will show them all!"

Tomorrow, in the boys' races, Ba-ee would skim down the track like a passing breeze, with Johnnie wearing his new beaded vest and leggings. There would be a crowd, a large, cheering crowd that would marvel at Ba-ee's speed, not seeing the twisted foot of the rider. Tomorrow was the day!

The fairgrounds were teeming with people and horses and dogs when Johnnie and his family arrived the next forenoon. They found an empty spot to pitch the cone-shaped tepee they had brought, and Johnnie tethered the old team that had drawn the wagon from the reservation. Laughing Fawn unpacked the huge Dutch oven and started the noon meal, but Johnnie was too excited to eat the fried potatoes and salt pork. Instead, he mounted Ba-ee and rode down into town, proud and self-conscious.

"The people like us, Ba-ee," he whispered in Arapaho, "but wait, just wait until this afternoon."

He passed an outdoor stand where brightly colored trinkets were displayed. He reined in and looked down at the baubles. In his pocket was a quarter. Pogy would like one of these treasures. He pointed to a small gold ring with a gay red stone.

"How much?" he asked shyly.

The girl at the stand smiled and held it out. "Fifteen cents," she said. "Do you want it?"

Johnnie handed her his coin. "I'll put it in my pocket," he said, eager to get back to the fairgrounds. Five-year-old Pogy would be very pleased to have the ring.

When the loud-speaker announced the boys' race, Johnnie urged Ba-ee into the crowd of ponies at the starting line. He was proud of his pet, for Ba-ee, instead of rearing and plunging and jostling his neighbors, stood quietly. It took several moments to arrange the group, because ponies kept breaking away. Each time, Ba-ee's ears twitched, and Johnnie could feel his body quivering, but he never left his place.

Then the starter raised his hand, warning them. The gun barked, and the race was on!

Events followed so swiftly that later Johnnie could never have told what happened. One moment he was on Ba-ee, and the next, he had slipped sidewise, clutching futilely at Ba-ee's long mane as he went over.

The pony, sensing something was wrong, slackened his pace. The other horses streaked by, while Johnnie slid to the ground, still clutching Ba-ee's mane.

In the grandstand he heard a girl scream, and he realized that more than two thousand eyes were on him. Ba-ee stood rigid, his eyes wild and eager, his breath coming in great gasps.

"Ba-ee!" The word was more agonized moan than anything else, as Johnnie sprang once more to the moist red back. Seizing Ba-ee's mane in trembling hands, he urged the horse forward.

By now the rest of the ponies had rounded the far end of the track. They were already halfway around by the time Ba-ee found his stride and flattened, his hoofs making swift music on the dusty track. Johnnie stretched out on his pet's neck, the skin on his face taut.

"It's all my fault, Ba-ee," he whispered hoarsely into the flying mane. "I'm only a clumsy cripple, and I've made you lose the race!"

The two of them raced on, the wretched boy and the straining horse, until the dust from the stragglers stung their faces and they became a part of the group that swept by the finishing point.

Johnnie did not check Ba-ee's speed. Instead, the two streaked on down the track, oblivious to the roaring crowd, oblivious to the dust and burning heat waves that rose from beneath Ba-ee's flying hoofs, oblivious to everything but crushing defeat.

Not until they had skimmed across the far end of the fairgrounds did Johnnie relax the speed of his pet. Behind him the band had burst into brilliant marching music, but Johnnie did not hear it. He heard nothing but the derisive voice of failure screaming at him.

Both were flecked with perspiration when they came to the road leading toward camp. Blindly, Johnnie turned the pony onto the highway. He had to escape the scene of his disgrace. He knew, deep inside, that his mother would be worrying about his racing away as he had done, but he was powerless to stop. He had to get away from the crowd!

Mile after mile they traveled in the still afternoon, Johnnie slumped dejectedly, scarcely noticing the heat that stung his back and arms, and the dust caked on his face. He was conscious of only one thing. He had failed! Through his clumsiness, he had lost the race! His splendid dreams were shattered, along with his pride. He dreaded the return of his family and the rest of the tribe day after tomorrow, for what could he say to them? He was thankful that tonight, at least, he would be alone.

It was early evening when he finally turned into the lane. How many times he and Ba-ee had ridden down this lane joyfully! Now, he had no eyes to see the green willows and graceful grasses. Life was very cruel, indeed, to snatch his meager victory from him so ruthlessly.

He led Ba-ee down to the river for a drink, and dipped his own dusty face into the waters along with his pet. It tasted warmish and flat to his tongue, and he rose, shaking the hair out of his eyes impatiently. Ba-ee drank on noisily, knowing nothing of the turmoil within his master's breast. It had been a big day for the pony, and he was content to relax by the river and fill his belly with clover.

Johnnie removed his beautiful leggings and jacket listlessly. A great tiredness swept over him. He stretched out on the rough blankets and sighed. It was lonely in the deserted camp, lonely and very, very quiet. Suddenly he longed for the return of his family, even though his brothers were sure to mock him. Anything would be better than this awful quiet, with only bitter memories to tantalize him.

His eyes closed wearily, and he slept. Outside, Ba-ee munched away busily, not knowing that today he had experienced defeat.

Pale moonlight was flooding the tepee when voices outside wakened Johnnie. He blinked dully, still half asleep. Then he heard his mother's voice, and it was frightened.

He sprang from the blankets. At the flap of the tepee he stopped short. The family was still in the wagon, gathered around his mother. She was holding Pogy, a struggling, gasping Pogy.

"What's wrong?" the boy said, fear clutching his heart.

"The ring," his mother said. "He has just swallowed the ring! It is caught in his throat! Oh—oh—" her voice ended in a moan.

"A doctor, we must have a doctor!" Johnnie said, and he thought of Ba-ee. "I will take Ba-ee and go for the doctor. There are no other horses in camp except those," and he pointed to the team, drooping in the shadows. "They are too slow. I will ride Ba-ee to the Government hospital for Dr. Gale."

He rushed across the clearing without waiting for an answer. Pogy was choking to death, and it was his fault! He had given him the ring only today!

He did not bother with reins, but flung himself on Ba-ee's startled back. The pony snorted in amazement, and plunged.

"Hurry!" Johnnie cried, digging his knees into Ba-ee's sides. "This is no game! We've got a job to do—a big job!"

The horse needed no second urging. In a clatter of hoofs the pair streaked down the moon-drenched lane. Johnnie's heart was in his mouth, and as he rode, he prayed. Pogy must not die! It was up to him to save his small brother's life!

There was no automobile in front of the small hospital. Johnnie's hope died. Suppose the doctor was not here! Suppose he was off on a call somewhere! What would he do then? He knocked frenziedly on the door. When no one answered, he flung it open and rushed in. A nurse was coming down the corridor, and behind her he could see Dr. Gale.

He felt weak with relief. In a flow of words he told them of Pogy's plight. The doctor's brow creased. "My car has a flat tire," he said. "How did you come? Did you ride a pony?"

Johnnie thought of Ba-ee, who had never known another rider, except Pogy. "My pony is wild," he said hesitantly, and then the vision of Pogy choking rose before him. "But you can handle him, sir," he went on quickly, afraid the doctor would refuse to come. "He is our only hope. Please ride him!"

The doctor looked at the nurse. She nodded and hurried out for his bag. "Put in an extra flashlight, Hodges," he called after her and started for the door. "Let me see the pony," he said. "I haven't ridden much lately, but I think I can manage."

He whistled when he saw Ba-ee standing by the porch, his sides streaked with foam. "No bridle?" he said. "how will I guide him?"

"Ba-ee knows the way, sir," Johnnie said, and went to his pet's head. "You must go home without me, Ba-ee," he said earnestly, taking the soft muzzle in his hand. "You must hurry home with the doctor."

The nurse was beside them now. Johnnie held out his hand for Dr. Gale to mount. Ba-ee quivered and stood still, while his strange new burden settled itself. The doctor reached for his bag.

"Find a bed for this young man, nurse," he said. "I'll be back when I can. Don't worry, lad," he told Johnnie, smiling grimly. "This horse is all right." He gave Ba-ee a vigorous slap. "Now let's get going, fellow." He leaned forward on Ba-ee's neck and waved back at Johnnie, staring dully after the fast retreating form of his pet.

If nothing happened, the doctor might reach camp in time. He cursed his selfishness in letting no one ride Ba-ee but Pogy. If the pony shied or ran away with Dr. Gale tonight, Johnnie could never forgive himself. It would be his fault if Pogy died.

He felt a hand on his arm. It was the nurse, coaxing him to come inside. "There's nothing you can do now," she said gently. "Come in and rest. Look, you are soaking wet with perspiration. You will catch cold."

Johnnie shook his head. "No thank you, ma'am. I must start for home. They might need me. I couldn't rest, not knowing."

The nurse started to protest, but something in the pinched face stopped her. "I think I understand," she said quietly. "But have faith, young man. Dr. Gale will arrive in time."

An hour later Johnnie was still swinging painfully down the highway. Never before had his lameness seemed so irksome as it did now. Every muscle strained to run to camp, yet here he was, struggling along at a snail's pace. He tried to keep from imagining what might be taking place at camp. Had the doctor arrived? Was he able to help Pogy? If his mother hadn't been worried about Johnnie's coming home alone today, they would still be in town, where there were plenty of doctors. Then Pogy would not be choking to death in the darkness of the camp.

Bitter pangs of conscience plagued the youth. He had been a fool. He had kept Ba-ee to himself; he had made such wild, crazy plans. How could he have hoped to win the races? He did not deserve to win them! He was selfish and vain. And now he was being punished—only it was Pogy who suffered, instead.

A sound came to him—a sound of swift hoofs.

He strained to see ahead into the moonlight night. Was it the doctor returning so soon? Had he been too late to do anything? Why was he coming away from camp so soon?

He stopped and waited as the hoofbeats became louder and Ba-ee appeared. Then they were beside him, the doctor and Ba-ee.

"Pogy?" he said, fearful.

The doctor handed him his bag. "Fit as a fiddle, young man, but I wasn't a moment too soon. Fine horse you have here."

Johnnie's knees felt strange. "Then he's all right?" he said, his voice a hoarse whisper. "Pogy is all right?"

"Sure thing." The doctor slid to the ground, letting out a small groan. "Haven't had a ride like that in years. I'll be stiff as a board tomorrow. Here, take this speed demon. You'll be wanting to get right back to camp." He shook his head as Johnnie started to protest. "No, I've had all I can take in one dose. The walk will do me good. But don't gallop. Horse needs a rest, I'd say."

Johnnie mounted Ba-ee in a daze. He was hardly conscious of waving good-by to the doctor and heading back for camp. Pogy was safe! He wasn't going to die. Ba-ee had saved his life!

Ba-ee turned into the home lane eagerly. The moon was riding low in the heavens by now, and the sagebrush had a silver radiance. Down by the river the crickets were sounding off.

Johnnie sighed deeply and ran his hand along

Ba-ee's foam-flecked neck. "Never mind the races, little cayuse," he whispered into the alert red ears. "There will be time for many more races, but, they do not matter. Pogy is alive."

A Filly Owns a Fella!

MATT ARMSTRONG

MA STOPPED Ramey at the door.

"Don't you dare take one step into this kitchen, young man, till you brush the snow off your feet," she said firmly.

Ramey's face glowed. "I haint comin' in, Ma," he cried out. "Just look at the snow, Ma! Boys, won't that old track be good for the races on the ice Satiddy, though!" He snatched up the broom from the corner of the stoop, then dropped it again. "Boys, won't little old Bonnie Bee show them slow-pokes a trot or two? . . . Here, Ma, take my books, please. I got to see is Bonnie all right. S'long, Ma."

Ma smiled indulgently. "Oh, you and that filly!" she said, and the fondness glowed like foxwood in her eyes. "But don't get so excited, Ramey. Just stand right there till I see can I find a Spy and a couple fresh fried-cakes for you and Bonnie."

He danced with impatience.

The filly rolled her eyes back at him and whinnied softly as he rushed into the box stall and slapped her sleek black rump. "It's snowin', Bonnie," he whispered. "And it's mild and the snow will pack jus' right Satiddy." He fed the apple to her, holding it in the palm of his hand as she nibbled daintily at it, while he ate his fried-cake from the other hand. "Gonna git you sharp-shod tomorry after four, Bonnie." Grabbing the fork, he hurriedly cleaned out the stable and spread fresh straw, breathing in the fine stuffy smell of the straw and the rich acrid aroma of the manure. "Now I got to go finish paintin' your sulky. S'long, Bonnie."

Stopping only long enough to make certain the barn door was closed tightly to keep the winter wind from Bonnie, he galloped his lanky legs down through the village, his heavy lumberman's rubbers thumping the soft new snow, the tassel of his red stocking cap flagging behind him, up the slope to the canal bridge and across to the Slabtown side. His father's shop faced the canal; the sign in big black letters over the doorway stated:

CARRIAGES—*Daniel Stone*—WAGONS

Pa didn't seem to be about, so pausing only for a moment to catch his wind and breathe in the smell of the fresh white oak shavings, he ran upstairs to where the ice-racing sulky waited for a final coat of yellow paint.

Footsteps below, and the sound of a voice,

stopped Ramey's brush. He listened, and Clem Beecher was saying: "Well, sir, Dan, I'm givin' you a chancet to pay off the five hundred you owe me, and I think you're foolish not to take it."

Clem Beecher owned the Beecher House, the brick Slabtown hotel down toward the river, across the market square. A trotting-horse man, Clem Beecher was.

"Clem, I can't take no chancet on losin' the filly, and that's all there is to it," Pa's voice rose up through the open trapdoor. Pa's voice sounded sort of tight and serious.

At the mention of the filly, Ramey held his breath.

For a long time there came no other sound.

Then Clem Beecher said: "Well, Dan, I'm a sucker and I know it, but I'm going to give you a bargain you can't refuse. . . . Dan, you won't bet me even, the filly ag'in' the five hundred you owe me, so here's what I'll do with you: We'll race three half-mile heats on Satiddy, your Bonnie Bee ag'in' my Gray Gander. Beat us, and you don't owe me a plugged nickel, understand; and if I should win, I'll still give you five hundred for the filly, provided you pay your debt with the spondulix. . . . How's that, Dan Stone? . . . Nell's bells, man, you can't lose. But you got to speak up quick. I can't be a sucker fer too long at a stretch."

Ramey's heart paced a two-eighteen mile.

Beecher added: "I sure got an awful hankerin' fer that little girl, Dan, to make such a sucker bet fer meself."

Pa's next words cut Ramey like a whiplash.

"Clem, you got me," Pa said hoarsely. "I can't turn that down. The way the carriage trade is right now, Harry only knows when I'll be able to pay you that five hundred, and it wouldn't be givin' you a fair shake to say no. It'll break the boy's heart if I lose the filly fer him, but I got to take a chancet. I got to, Clem. A man that's a man has got to play fair with his creditors, too. . . . I'll take that bet, Clem Beecher. And by Godfrey, we'll trim the pants off that gray colt of yourn."

Clem Beecher guffawed. "Mebbe," he said. "Mebbe."

"She's slick as an eel, Clem."

"She sure is, Dan. Sure is. . . . Well, let's slip down and have one on the house to sort of seal the bargain. What d'ya say?"

The door-hinges creaked. Footsteps faded.

After a while Ramey looked at the floor, and there was a yellow pool where his paintbrush had dripped, and there were streaks of paint on his lumberman's sock.

The river shimmered under the bright winter sun like a white blanket strewn with a million jewels. There was no wind. The crowd, folks from town in their Sunday-go-to-meeting clothes, farmers and trotting-horse men in their fur coats and fur caps, idle fishermen from Port Martin at the mouth of the river, and Slabtowners in their mackinaws and inevitably pulled-up hip boots, milled and stamped and joked with each other as they massed about the point of the kite-shaped track—the V-point that was the starting and finishing point—a hard track of snow, packed over eighteen inches of river ice. From the crowd excitement arose like heat-waves rising from a wood-stove. Weather clear; track fast.

Ramey, walking Bonnie up and down outside the rim of the crowd, paused to watch, feeling the good excitement warming him as the five horses in the first heat of the two-thirty trot or pace emerged near him and wheeled for the start. His spine tingled. He waited, clinging tightly to Bonnie's halter-rope, as the trotters vanished again in the crowd; he heard Carson Miller's foghorn voice yell, *"Go,"* and knew it was a start.

"Pretty soon now, Bonnie," he whispered in the ear of his three-year-old. "Guess you'll show that Gray Gander hoss what a pair of heels looks like, eh? Boys—"

The filly twitched an understanding ear.

Far up at the head of the long starting straight-away, beyond the crowd, he saw the horses winging high, wide and handsome around the arc that formed the upper end of the kite. And at that moment he heard Carson Miller again calling through his megaphone from the judges' stand: "Get them hosses ready for the special. Bring in the Gray Gander and that Bonnie Bee hoss."

"Now, boy, don't you be frettin'," Pa said as they hitched the filly to the sulky. "Your Pa'll bring the girl in a-sailin'."

Ramey gulped hard. His pa looked mighty big and strong and powerful in his khaki jacket and fur cap, with the brown goggles stuck up on his brow. "Sure thing, Pa. I haint frettin' none. Little old Bonnie'll trim that gray hoss. She's got to, Pa."

"All we need is the breaks, son," Pa said. Pa's eyes were hard and serious.

It was a good start.

Ramey elbowed his way through the crowd to the finish-line and watched with galloping heart as the two horses flew into sight around the distant turn and pounded down the long homestretch toward him. The excitement made him clench his fists and curl his toes in his rubbers. He thrilled to the sound of the crowd around him, to the growing mutter as the horses flashed nearer and nearer, to the full-throated roar of approval as the little black filly flew across the finish-line a length to the good.

Pa winked, but neither said a word one way or the other, as they unhitched. Ramey spread a blue blanket over his filly, and led her for a cooling-out walk.

But in the second heat tragedy struck.

Waiting again at the finish-line, Ramey didn't see what happened, didn't know until afterward. All he knew was that suddenly the Gray Gander horse appeared around the turn and pounded down the stretch and across the finish-line—alone. Ramey felt sick. Like a shot he was through the crowd and running toward the arc of the track. Halfway, he met Pa, walking and leading the filly. Somehow—struck a chunk of ice, Pa thought—the sulky had bounced, and the filly reared, dumping him backward to the ice.

"And here's the worst of it, son," Pa said. "Look here!"

His right wrist was puffing. It was purple.

"Busted," Dan Stone said.

Father and son looked at each other. It hurt Ramey to see the terrible agony in pa's eyes, agony that he knew was more than the mere physical pain of a broken arm. He had never seen fear in Pa's eyes before.

Pa fumbled with his good hand and bit off a chew of tobacco.

"By Godfrey," Pa said in a whisper. "By the Godfrey—"

Blinking hard, Ramey blanketed the filly, then to keep his heart from overflowing put his arms tight about her neck. She was trembling. He walked her down back of the crowd and back again to where Pa still waited.

"Why don't you go get your arm fixed, Pa?" Ramey said.

Pa shook his head. "It's all right, son. . . . After a while."

Their eyes met again.

Ramey said: "Pa, I'll handle her in the last heat."

Pa shook his head. "Godfrey, I wish you could, boy. I wish you could, but you haint heavy enough in the behind to hold 'er down on the turn, Ramey.

Wouldn't stand a mud turtle's chancet. . . . By Godfrey, boy, it looks like we're licked."

Ramey bit his lip. "Pa," he said grimly, "I'm gonna handle her. We haint gonna give Bonnie to Clem Beecher 'thout a race."

"What you talkin' about?" Pa said quickly, eyes bugging.

"I'm talkin' about the bet you made with Mr. Beecher. I was upstairs paintin' the sulky, and I heard you and him makin' it up 'twixt you."

"Oh. . . . Zat so?"

"Yessir."

"You heard that, and didn't put up no holler? You didn't tell your Ma nor nothin'?" Amazement filled Pa's face. He spat a brown stream on the snow and wiped his mustache. "You had spunk enough to let 'er ride? . . . Well, sir, if that don't beat the band."

Ramey reached out and touched Pa's coat-sleeve. "Sure thing, Pa. I know you couldn't turn down a chancet like that. If you hadn't took him up, I'd of thought you didn't have no faith in Bonnie Bee. And she just proved you were right by beatin' Gray Gander, didn't she, Pa? And she can do it again."

Pa's eyes glistened. He laid a tender hand on Ramey's shoulder. "By Godfrey, son, you're a real Stone," he said hoarsely. "For a thirteen-year-old, you got grit. You sure have. . . . Take the ribbons, son, and good luck."

Pa headed for the refreshment stand to swallow a couple of stiff coffee royals.

He hurried back when Carson Miller called for the final heat. "Watch out for Beecher's tricks, boy," he whispered. "He's a hard man in a hoss-race." He loosed the filly's head, and Ramey eased her, dancing and chewing at her bit, onto the track.

As the two horses minced side by side out to wheel for the start, Clem Beecher worked his cigar-stub over to the corner of his mouth and threatened Ramey: "Now, fella, when you hear me holler, 'Look out, boys—here I come' you'd best pull over to the side and let me pass, for when I come a-chargin', I don't fool around. I'd drive this hoss through hell and high water if I had to." He scowled hard at Ramey.

Ramey's stomach tightened, but without an answering word he eased the black filly around and clucked her into a slow trot. Head and head they crossed the starting-line. Then Carson Miller yelled, *"Go!"* Ramey flicked his whip in the air, and at once the snow beneath him began to slide out from under with terrifying speed. He gained a short lead and held Bonnie close to the inside of the track up the straightaway, then gritted his teeth and held her tight to make the semi-circular turn without skidding wide into the path of the gray horse. A quick sidewise glimpse showed him the gray horse's head near his shoulder. He set his teeth hard and held the filly tight. A steady stream of ice- and snow-pellets beat against his face like BB shot. He held his lead.

Then Beecher made his move. Ramey heard

his yell as they were about to swing into the home-stretch, and from the corner of his eye he saw the big gray colt charging right at him from the outside of the track. Before he could shake the filly out, the Beecher horse was at his shoulder and going past like a locomotive under full steam. Beecher yelled again. He waved his whip. As he drew alongside the black filly's shoulder, the whip flicked like a snake's tongue, and suddenly Bonnie broke. She jumped and tried to rear. Ramey sawed on the reins. He thought that Beecher's whip had struck Bonnie's tender nose, but he couldn't be certain. By the time he managed to pull his filly down to a steady trot again, the broad back of Clem Beecher was riding high a good three lengths ahead.

Ramey sobbed. Then, *"Bonnie!"* he screamed. "Bonnie! Git outa here!" Lightly he flicked his whip-tip against the filly's flank, and she was off in pursuit. And now again he could feel the life in her, could thrill to the great heart and the supple strength in her as she surged ahead, her tiny feet flashing like beads of quicksilver down the stretch. Steadily now, she gained. Cut the lead to two lengths. . . . To one. Once more Ramey touched her with the whip as the gathering roar of the crowd swept into his ears, driven by the terrific rush of air as he and Bonnie pulled up inch by inch alongside the hard-driving gray colt. Beecher's huge red face seemed close enough to touch.

Ramey couldn't be certain just when they flashed across the finish-line. Nor was he certain how they crossed it.

When at last he got the filly pulled down to a walk and swung her around, he saw Carson Miller beckoning from the judges' stand. Pa took the filly's head. Clem Beecher handed his lines to his hostler, Vinegar Charley. Then together Ramey and Beecher walked to face the judges.

"Mr. Stone," Miller said, "what happened up there on the turn?"

Ramey looked at Beecher, who studied the snow at his feet.

"Why, nothing, sir," Ramey said clearly. "The filly broke, that's all."

Beecher looked up suddenly at Ramey, eyes puzzled.

"Then you have no claim to lodge?"

"No, sir, Mr. Miller."

Miller shrugged his shoulders and turned into a huddle with the other two judges; and for that awful endless moment Ramey's heart bounced and leaped in his chest like a frog in an empty rain-barrel. Then the judge faced the crowd and announced: "The winner of the special, ladies and gentlemen, is Mr. Clement Beecher's good gray hoss, Gray Gander. . . . And now will you bring in them two-thirty hosses, please, for the next heat."

Faintly, from miles off across the great white river, Ramey heard Clem Beecher's voice: "Too bad, fella—too bad—" Then the voice faded and Ramey's world faded with it. He saw only a blurry view of Pa's stricken face, heard only a blurry sound that might have been Pa's voice, and with the weight on his heart, the feel of Pa's hand on his shoulder made no difference. He didn't even look for Bonnie. All he knew was that Bonnie was gone. His lovely little filly was gone. And all at once the hard-driving devil-may-care driver in him vanished, and he was a thirteen-year-old boy again, a broken-hearted little boy; and when he could see through his blurred eyes, he was through the crowd and tearing up the Slabtown road to the canal bridge on the dead run, and across the bridge and into the hot, cozy kitchen, sobbing his heart out on a broad, warm bosom that smelled of fresh-baked bread; and he was tasting in his mouth the taste of salt tears, and Ma's hand was on his head pressing him close to her, and Ma's sweet voice was saying over and over: "There now. . . . There now. . . . There now."

"Where you goin', son?" Ramey stopped in the shop doorway, looking back at his father. Pa was looking straight at him with a kindness in his eyes that made a liar out of the tone he used.

Ramey didn't speak, so Pa asked again: "Beecher's barn?"

Ramey said: "Yes, sir."

Pa pulled at his mustache.

"Beecher tells me you been comin' down there curryin' Bonnie and feedin' her apples fer two weeks now, ever since the— Well, ever since. That right?"

"He said I could, Pa. I ast him."

"Sure, son. But don't you think y'ought to try

to forget the filly? You'd better stay away from her."

"But Pa, she sort of expecks me. She'd miss me."

"You'll both get over it, son. You got to get used to being without her, see?"

Ramey swallowed. "Don't seem's if I could, Pa." His mouth felt dry.

Pa suddenly looked mad.

"I'm telling you, Ramey, to stay away from that barn. Now you git that hoss out of your head. Understand?"

Ramey toed a great B on the floor.

"Yes, sir," he said.

He wandered over to the bench and began fooling with a stick of white oak. It was a stick he'd put away weeks before, to make a shinny-stick from, but he had forgotten it. Hadn't felt like playing shinny lately. From the corner of his eye he watched Pa fidgeting on the stool before the wood-stove. He guessed this idleness—Pa still had his broken arm in a sling—was sort of getting him down. Always liked to work, Pa did.

Pa came over.

"You know I don't want to be hard on you, boy," he said. "Tell the truth, what I started out to tell you was that I'd as soon you'd stay clear of Beecher's barn for a while anyway, because Vinegar Charley's on a spree. Day before yesterday when Beecher shipped his hosses up the river, he left Charley home—sent Sam instead—and Charley's sore. He's shootin' off his mouth about what he'll do. He's an ugly-enough fellow when he's sober, but when he hits the booze, there haint nothing he wouldn't do. Just as well to stay away from there, aside from the hoss end of it, Ramey. See, son?"

Ramey said, sadly: "Sure, Pa." He couldn't work up any interest in Vinegar Charley and his threats.

The fire-bell over town clanged. Together they rushed to the door. From over town they heard the higher-pitched bells of the fire-wagon, coming closer, and closer, and suddenly the big white team dashed into view around the corner, tore across the canal bridge and vanished toward Slabtown. Someone yelled: "Hey, it's Beecher's barn!"

Ramey grabbed Pa's arm. "Bonnie! Bonnie'll git burnt up! Oh, Bonnie!" he screamed; and before Pa could stop him, he was off around the corner of the building and tearing down across the market square like a scared cottontail. Smoke filled the sky behind the hotel. In the gathering dusk of the late afternoon, a red glow made fantastic, twisting ogres in the smoke. Ramey squirmed through the crowd and leaped the hose-lines. Halfway back the lane alongside the hotel, he ran into Clem Beecher.

"Whoa there, fella," Clem yelled, and grabbed his arm.

Ramey panted: "Lemme go, Mr. Beecher. Got to git Bonnie out."

"You can't do it, fella. You're crazy." Sweat shone on Beecher's round face. "The hull back end's afire, and it's gettin' to the haymow. Git out front, fella. Chase yourself."

Ramey, sobbing, squirmed free and ran to the barn.

At the open door he paused only long enough to take one deep breath; then he was inside, bending low under the ceiling of smoke, and racing toward Bonnie's stall in the middle of the barn. The back end of the barn was solid flame. It was like running into an open furnace. Bonnie pranced and jerked at her halter-rope as he slid in beside her. Baring her teeth, she screamed in terror.

"Bonnie," Ramey called, fumbling at the knot. "Quiet, Bonnie." He used a few precious seconds to pat her hot neck. She calmed slightly. He threw his jacket over her head, held it with one hand under her jaw, and with the halter-rope in the other hand, backed her out of the stall and headed her toward the door. He longed to run, but he forced himself to walk, holding his breath as long as possible, breathing with his nose close to his shoulder when he had to, and dragging his weight to keep the filly from going into a fit of plunging, suicidal hysteria. The smoke was thick and sharp in his nostrils. The heat crinkled his face. Somehow he found the door again, and dashed outside, with the flames from the dry hay overhead leaping and roaring at the filly's heels.

In the lane Clem Beecher grabbed and held him until he got his breath. "You all right, fella?" Clem asked. His voice was anxious.

Ramey gasped. His face and his hands hurt. "Sure thing. . . . So's Bonnie." He grinned up at the frightened face of Clem Beecher.

"Good gosh, fella," Clem said hoarsely, "you were crazy to do that. Another minute, and you'd never got out. Good gosh almighty, fella!" He stared at Ramey for a long time, and the amazement and awe stayed in his face as he fussed over him and led him around the edge of the crowd to the carriage-shop.

Ramey led the filly into the shop—began wiping her down.

Beecher looked thoughtful.

"Filly hurt any, fella?" he asked.

Ramey patted her nose. "No, sir," he said. "Mane's singed a little, I guess. Still scairt, though." He could feel the filly trembling under his hand.

Beecher stared at them, the boy and the filly, snuggling close like sweethearts. He worked up a good stiff scowl. "Well, sir," he said after a while, "I'm sure glad my hosses was shipped out day before yesterday. My good hosses, that is." His voice was very gruff. "Seems to me, fella, that you went to a mighty lot of trouble to save a sliver of useless hossflesh like that spoiled black brat. She haint worth it. I've tried fer two weeks to handle 'er, but I can't do a thing with the clown. Most empty-headed hoss I ever had to feed."

Ramey listened, but kept wiping.

"Can't think when I was so disappointed in a hoss," Beecher went on. "She haint worth a wooden nickel to me."

Ramey straightened. The insulting words fired his backbone.

"She's the best filly in the world, Mr. Beecher," he said.

"Best hayburner, don't you mean?" Beecher guffawed.

"She is, eh? Well, I'll tell you something, Mr. Beecher: my filly can beat that Gray Gander horse of yours six days in the week and twicet on Sundays, and you know it."

Beecher grinned. "*Whose* filly?"

"My—" Ramey shut his mouth. "Guess I forgot," he said lamely.

Beecher spoke quickly. "You're right, fella. She's your filly. I left my barn afire back there because I wanted to let you know that she is your filly, allus has been and allus will be, if the way she acts means anything. Anyway, fella, you earned the right to the girl all over again back there at the barn. . . . Besides that, though, if you'd've claimed foul that day on the river, she never would've been in my barn. She don't belong to me—she's your filly, all right."

Ramey stiffened.

"You don't have to give her to me, Mr. Beecher."

Beecher snorted. "Me give anything away? No, fella, I haint quite that soft. I'll do anything—nigh on—to win a hoss-race; but so fur, I haint a hoss-thief. I thought I wanted this filly, but I know now she's no good. Anyway, I got no barn to keep her in if I did want her." He found a cigar in his shirt pocket and lit it. "Next time we race on the river, we'll glue your Pa in the sulky seat, and then mebbe when Cars Miller sees me usin' my head on the turn, we'll have a little fun out of it. Your Pa'd never stand quiet like you did. He'd holler his head off. Guess your pa's bringin' you up too danged honest to be a good hoss man. . . . Guess a good hoss-handler's got to be part hoss thief."

He blew his nose hard. Ramey thought he must be catching cold.

"Well, don't stand there like a wooden Indian," Beecher said then. "Git that no-good filly across that bridge and into her barn. I can't waste any more time standin' around like this when my barn's a-burnin'. Mebbe the house is afire by now." He waddled away, but at the door he glanced backward. "Then I got to find that Vinegar Charley. Just want to ask him a few questions about this-here fire. Just out o' curiosity." He glared hard at Ramey. "Don't stand there gawpin'. Git that filly home. You hear me?"

Ramey swallowed. "Yes, sir," he said.

Beecher slammed the door.

Alone, Ramey's heart spilled over. Sobbing, he threw his arms around the filly's neck and wept there helplessly, weak-kneed in his overpowering happiness; feeling the grand feel of her hide against his cheek, reveling in the beautiful smell of her, every inch of his being thrilling anew to the life that rippled along the arched neck of the filly—*his* filly.

Stand to Horse

FAIRFAX DOWNEY

LIEUTENANT FERDINAND JONES, Field Artillery, was suffering the consequences of having routed a stable sergeant out for reveille. Not even a world war justified that. Now as he dragged himself on toward the stable through the sunshine of Virginia, the whole harrowing scene flashed back through his mind.

As painfully green as unripe apples taken internally, he had made the mistake of trying to cover it up by super-activity. Hearing sincere snores proceeding from a tent two minutes before assembly, he had thrust open the flap and commanded:

"Turn out there. Reveille's blown. Snap out of it!"

No answer from the heap of blankets. No obedience, unless you consider the lieutenant's command had included, "Cease snoring."

" 'Snap out of it,' I said."

"Aw, go to——."

"Here! This is an officer speaking."

Stable Sergeant Mike McRuddy was an old soldier. But this was the limit. He had suffered much in this war army that was so new it squeaked. So the heap of blankets responded very sleepily and sorely—

"Well, this is a stable sergeant sleeping."

"Makes no difference. Out with you and into line."

"Sir, does the lieutenant know I was up four times last night with a sick horse?"

"That's an old one. Line up or be reported to the colonel."

So Mike McRuddy, his Irish so far up it broke an altitude record, had had to rush his small bristling body into his uniform and fall in. The amusement of the battery at the spectacle had spread through the regiment much to the anger of the butt. And Jones had soon become aware of the enormity of his violation of army tradition. Good stable sergeants should not be required to do anything—except be good stable sergeants.

Shuddering at the memory of the scene, the lieutenant passed the gun park with a longing look and entered a long low stable building over the door of which was the legend, "Battery B." It seemed to blur before his eyes into "All hope abandon, ye who enter here."

Grooming already was in progress. In two long rows of stalls the battery's horses were undergoing the systematic back-scratching, dusting, massaging and pedicuring which the army rigorously prescribes. Some of the nags did not seem half to appreciate the attention they were getting. To put it mildly, they fidgeted. Some laid back their ears in a most malicious manner; others snorted and gave dirty looks with the whites of their eyes. The soldiers doing the grooming—most of them recruits with which a skeleton regular army outfit had been brought to war strength—were as a rule nervous about their task. Only the farm boys among them were entirely at their ease. Supervising, the veteran non-coms moved about among the men of their sections. Lieutenant Jones entered, young, sturdy but not eager.

Presiding over it all stood the small but formidable figure of Stable Sergeant McRuddy. He bristled with vengefulness. The three chevrons over a horse head, the insignia of his rank, seemed fairly to champ out from each arm at the newcomer, on whom he bent such a black-browed look as is given a tardy and inept pupil reaching school. The recipient quailed visibly and forgot to answer a casual salute.

"Everything all right, Sergeant?" he inquired apprehensively.

"As right as it can be with them boneracks the Remount wished on us," the stable sergeant sniffed.

"I meant comparatively," the lieutenant hedged. "Well, let's feed 'em up and do the best we can."

"With what particular—sor?"

"Oh, the usual ration and—" the words of the bugle call ran through the lieutenant's head: "And give your poor horses some hay and some corn," and he added, "try some corn."

"Since when are we bein' issued corn?" There was a leer on the sergeant's face. The officer caught it.

"I was only joking," he put in quickly and hastily walked away.

Now Second Lieutenant Ferdinand Jones was almost as ignorant of horses as he was of ostriches; more, they struck terror in his bosom. He wished to Heaven they were one and all tractors. His only consolation in the field artillery was the guns, and the ranking lieutenant in the battery had been assigned to their care, as the usage is. As the next in rank, Jones got the horses and there was nothing to do but bluff it through. Colonel McCaskey had threatened that any officer, greenness notwithstanding, who failed to hold down his job was due for transfer to the home guard before the regiment sailed. The colonel spoke like a first primer since the occasion when an officer had given the alibi that he had not understood an order the colonel gave.

"This, gent-le-men, is war," the C. O. had declared slowly. "I will not tol-er-ate ignor-ance as an excuse."

So Lieutenant Jones bluffed and, due to rare luck, got away with it.

He walked down the aisle inspecting the grooming, wishing the ordeal over. Any moment someone might ask him something. Horrors! Here came a recruit now.

"Please, sir," begged the recruit, almost tearfully, "I can't make this horse lift up his back foot."

"Use a little force, man," the lieutenant advised gruffly, though his heart bled for the youth.

"Please show me how, sir," the recruit pleaded.

Here was a fix. Probably the beast kicked or tried to sit in your lap when you picked up one foot, Jones reflected. Still he must try. He felt the eyes of the stable sergeant boring into his back. He advanced gingerly.

Then, in the nick of time, came Stable Orderly Farris to his rescue. Farris was a good looking, intelligent young soldier who knew horses.

"Don't bother the lieutenant!" Farris said. "Here, like this."

He spoke to the horse and patted him on the haunch, gradually sliding his hand down to the fetlock. Then with the pressure of his shoulder he threw the horse's weight off that foot and raised it easily for cleaning.

Saved! Jones sighed with relief and Stable Sergeant McRuddy moved off, obviously disappointed. But he was not to be balked. He returned to the attack. A vindictive strain seemed to urge him to bring about the downfall of the tyro officer. In a loud, coldly calculating voice, he remarked—

"Here's a case of what I'd call thrush, lieutenant."

Thrush? Thrush? The brain of Lieutenant Ferdinand Jones spun in an agony of effort. He'd thought it was a bird. Obviously it was something horses had, though. Thrushes sang, didn't they? And—

he racked his brain for a hint from "The Care of the Horse"—and thrush had something to do with frogs. Ah! Undoubtedly a frog in the throat.

"Hm. Has the horse seemed at all hoarse lately, Sergeant?" the lieutenant inquired solicitously. "Er—that is, have you happened to hear him—er—neigh?"

An hour later, the unfortunate Jones had learned that thrush is a disease of the frog or horny pad in the center of the sole of a horse's foot. The knowledge came too late, for what might classically be called the blatt had driven the unhappy officer from the stable.

The black cloud was found to assay a silver lining. Rumors of the debacle reached the ears of the battery commander who relieved Jones from Department B which has charge of the horses. Though not daring to confess to the bluff he had been throwing in matters equine, the lieutenant accepted gun duty with great joy.

But the vengeance of Stable Sergeant Mike McRuddy had not had its fill. What had passed was only short rations. Those who think of the vendetta as peculiarly Italian fail to reckon with the sensibilities of the Celt. Thus entered upon the stage, as instrument of revenge, that mouse-colored charger widely known as Nemmy, short for Nemesis.

Nemmy was one of the worst atrocities the Remount Service ever inflicted on an outfit. The eagle eyes in the wise and wizened face of Stable Sergeant McRuddy singled him out in the draft of horses that brought the regiment up to war strength and he claimed him at once for purposes of sweet revenge.

The outward semblance of Nemmy was not such bad news. The steed stood high—sixteen hands—and he was structurally stout. But the way he showed the white of the eye that wasn't wall, the irritable switching of his tail and the room the other horses gave him were storm signs to the initiate.

No sooner was Nemmy on the Battery "B" picket line than McRuddy made occasion to remark casually to the battery commander:

"Here's a good mount for Lieutenant Jones, sor. It's a heavy man he is and the horse he has is too light and slow."

"All right," that officer agreed. "I'll assign him."

So it happened that the striker of Lieutenant Ferdy Jones led up for mounted drill that afternoon a strange and awesome beast in place of the docile nag that had previously served.

"There's a good new mount for you, Mr. Jones," the B. C. called over.

Nothing could be done about it then. Catching the glance of the lurking McRuddy, Ferdy knew that retribution was on the way and coming fast. Would that furious little Irishman never forgive and forget?

"Stand to horse," came the command to the battery.

As one man, the battery did. No, not as one man. As all but one man. Nemmy wouldn't be stood to. When his rider tried to assume a military position at his side, the charger sidled around. With a stern hold on the bridle, the lieutenant shifted too. They went around and around. It began to look like a merry-go-round.

"Sure, he's trying to catch the brass ring," McRuddy remarked audibly from the picket line.

"Mount."

Up swung drivers and cannoneers. For Ferdy, easier said than done. Nemmy nipped at him playfully and smote him with his tail, the while he absolutely refused to be scaled. The battery rolled off. When Jones got the creature cornered against the side of the stable, Nemmy coyly leaned hard against the man on his near side. At last Jones vaulted into the saddle and they were off.

They certainly were off. They flew past the battery. At the drill field, Jones got him turned around and they passed the battery just as fast in the opposite direction. After three more such passages, they arranged to drill with the battery. In the lieutenant's ears was ringing a cry he could have sworn he heard the stable sergeant give the last time he had hurtled up to the picket lines—"Try puttin' him in reverse, sor!"

Goaded into desperation, Jones at last had put the spurs to his mount during the drill maneuvers, and Nemmy, after turning his head and giving his rider a look of pained surprise, had become peaceful. It worked so well that fifteen minutes later when the charger showed signs of unrest, the lieutenant scratched enthusiastically again.

From behind him came a stern and awful voice.

"Young man," Colonel McCaskey rumbled, "there are bet-ter ways of man-a-ging a horse than digg-ing spurs into him. Spur him a-ga-in and you are re-lieved!"

Then Nemmy bolted. The Battery was ordered in forthwith by the colonel.

Excitement ran through the ranks like wildfire. What was up? Was something doing at last, were they off for France? Or was this just another one of those outbuilding rumors?

No, it was. It was the real thing! Orders came through thick and fast. Entrainment for personnel. Guns to be left—new ones over there. Horses?

No one in all the—the Field Artillery asked that last question more anxiously than Lieut. Ferdy Jones. His brain throbbed with hopes and fears. Perhaps the horses would be left behind, too, and new mounts would be obtained in France where men—and possibly horses—are proverbially polite. Perhaps, if they took the nags with them, there might come a Heaven-sent opportunity to push that mouse-colored monster overboard. Perhaps the horses might sail on another boat and be torpedoed all hands and hooves being rescued, Lieutenant Jones patriotically hoped, except Nemmy.

The orders realized the third case—in part, and Ferdy Jones breathed easier for a spell.

But only for a brief space. The figurative bomb burst when Captain Leonard of Battery B assembled his officers for assignment of the details in the sailing orders.

"Jones, you'll have to take our horse detail," he

said. "Sorry, but Hall here is transferred to the staff. You'll be all right, though. Sergeant McRuddy will be along and save you any trouble."

The miserable Jones could only gasp. Fate had socked him below the belt. Through his buzzing head kept running the phrase, "Lost at sea. Lost at sea."

Through the black encircling gloom, he could only discern one tiny ray of brightness. Maybe McRuddy and Nemmy, too, would get very seasick.

And then there was Farris, the stable orderly. That friendly and helpful young man might be his salvation in some measure.

"How about Farris?" Jones asked.

"——shame," the B. C. grumbled. "Got to lose him. He's had an application in for a commission for some time. Just got it. Glad for his sake. Good man."

The sturdy frame of Lieutenant Jones sagged woefully. Without, someone was heard whistling cheerily, "It's a Long Way to Tipperary." Unnecessarily cheerily, even in the event of the sailing orders. Surely it was McRuddy.

"Sunk without a trace," moaned the unhappy Jones.

But the attention of the others was on a headquarters orderly who had just entered.

"This is fair enough," the battery commander grinned. "Jones, you go with us after all. Farris is assigned back to us as a second loot. Of course, he's the logical man for the horse detail."

A bugler blew "Stables" out of tune.

To Ferdy Jones just then it sounded like the music of the heavenly choir.

The swirl of events which followed saw the —th Field Artillery in France and rushing through a brief period of training. There was no time for more than a brief one. The critical days of October, 1918, were at hand and outfits were badly needed to pinch-hit in the line.

"Gentlemen," Captain Leonard of Battery "B" declared to his officers, "as soon as that slow freight of a cattle boat gets across with our plugs, we're off for the front."

The heart of Lieut. Ferdy Jones, accompanying others, rose up, though with a tempered joy. Nemmy would be coming.

Next day a train pulled into the training base. But it was all *hommes* and no *chevaux*. The details rejoined their batteries but never a horse.

"They took 'em all away from us, sir," Farris explained to the B. C. "Sorry. Got almost all the nags across in good shape. They said we'd be issued new mounts nearer at hand. Probably never see our own."

"——uva note," swore Captain Leonard. "That's the army for you."

But the spirit of Lieutenant Jones sang a pæan of joy with variations. Farewell, a long farewell to Nemmy, that fiend in horse's form.

Again the swift swirl of events. The regiment entrained for the front via a remount depot where trained horses, previously shipped across, would be given them.

Detrainment. A rush for the corral. A battle royal between the battery commanders, seconded by stable sergeants, to obtain the best allotment of horses for the outfit of each.

"Recognize any of our old plugs in this bunch?" Captain Leonard inquired of his trusty assistant.

"No, sor," Mike McRuddy replied disappointedly. "But wait!"

The little Irishman dived into a fighting group of horses on one line.

"My ch'ice, my ch'ice!" he fairly screeched. "I chooses this here gray for "B" battery!"

He returned capering, leading his prize, a lofty, mouse-colored charger.

"It's Lieutenant Jones's horse, sor," he rejoiced, his eyes twinkling with sinister delight.

It was indeed Nemmy. By an odd quirk of fate —if it was that—the steed had come on through to the remount depot from the port in advance of all his mates. Probably he had been shoved into the last car of a departing train soon after he had debarked.

The reunion between Nemmy and Ferdy was a touching sight. At least it seemed to touch Sergeant McRuddy.

"It's in luck you are, sor," he chuckled diabolically to his victim when the meeting took place at the picket line. "Not another soul in the regiment got back his old mount, savin' the Colonel, and he's all for ridin' in his autymobile."

Jones quailed under the gaze of the wall off-eye of Nemmy. Horses seldom give signs of recognition and perhaps the signs that Nemesis gave were not such. But they were clearly signs of antipathy. He snorted, curled back his upper lip and made a gesture of contempt with his tail.

Many deeds of heroism went unrewarded by a medal in the Great War. Of such was the mounting up of Lieutenant Jones on Nemmy when the regiment pulled out the next morning, for the poor young man was terrified. Nothing untoward befell, however. Nemmy was not himself. It had been a tough voyage across and he had been seasick.

By slow, short marches the regiment proceeded. Strong as was the need of haste, Colonel McCaskey was too old a campaigner to wear down soft horses. The fighting was opening up farther ahead in the Argonne, and apparently the trench staff was through for a time. One of the prime characteristics of field artillery is mobility. The old colonel having come far for a scrap was not going to break down on the fringe of one.

Condition the horses—spare them as much as possible. Those were the strict orders. None was more zealous in carrying them out than Lieutenant Ferdinand Jones. His energy and enthusiasm became a by-word. He seemed never to be mounted. His horse was always led, while he encouraged the men, cannoneers and drivers, by trudging along the column with them. Occasionally he would offer his mount to a footsore cannoneer, but the brave fellow would look up, then pull himself together, refuse with thanks and drag himself on.

The implacable McRuddy rode along the column of Battery "B," watching the adjustment of collars, seeing that saddle blankets did not slip back. He loved horses, did the little Irish stable sergeant. If he loved anything better it was an enemy. Therefore his most triumphant discovery of the march was not a piece of harness galling a trusty wheel horse, but the spectacle of Lieut. Ferdinand Jones seated at the roadside, dragging off a muddy boot to bind up a raw heel.

Poor Jones meekly suffered the leer he drew. Having once violated the sanctity of a stable sergeant's slumbers and been officious, he was determined to eat humble pie until forgiven. He did not know than an Irishman forgives easiest the enemy who fights back best.

So went the hike until a November day when Colonel McCaskey, charging up and down the column of the regiment in his automobile, ordered all moderation be forgotten and the horses pushed to the limit to bring the regiment to the front. To the ears of the old man had come a most disquieting rumor. It contained a hint of an impending truce. Thunderation! The war was about to die on him while he was still out of range.

The rumor spread. Drivers leaned forward in their saddles, horses strained their traces into taut lines, cannoneers, lightening the carriages of their weight and themselves of equipment, trotted alongside tugging at the wheel spokes in rough spots of the road. Lieutenant Jones mounted Nemmy, who stepped along friskily.

And so the —th Field Artillery plunged through the devastation of the Argonne Forest, and the next morning unlimbered and went into action with all twenty-four guns, swelling the roaring symphony of sound about them.

Colonel McCaskey, now horsed instead of limousined, trotted up to the observation post where Captain Leonard of Battery "B" was directing fire, assisted by Lieut. Ferdy Jones, the latter mounted on Nemmy, being about to ride back to the battery position. In the colonel's pocket were orders which confirmed that rumor of a truce—cease firing at 11 A.M. until further orders. That he transmitted privately to Captain Leonard.

With the men of the B. C. detail stood Stable Sergeant McRuddy glowering. "To see the fun," as he put it, he had left his place at the horse lines and joined the detail. He had no business there. And the worm had turned at last and told him so —the worm being none other than Lieutenant Jones.

"Well, we have fired at least," the colonel growled distinctly. "But think of never getting closer to the real front than two miles before"— the colonel ended in a burst of fancy cussing.

Then that old warrior grinned philosophically.

"For half a cent, I'd ride up," he chuckled and jokingly spurred his horse in the direction of the rattle of machine guns.

Colonel McCaskey wheeled back, but the

mounted man who had dashed out after his lead did not. A mouse-colored projectile with a clinging rider sped down a shelled road straight for the front lines. It was Nemmy—and Ferdy.

Stable Sergeant Mike McRuddy watched them go, aghast. He nursed his right hand which stung from a blow on a horse's haunch. And he whispered to himself contritely—

"Hivven rest his soul!"

Artillery fire seemed to be swelling to a crescendo. So did the stuttering of the machine guns and irregular, distant plop of the rifles.

Down the road tore Nemmy, the bit in his teeth, a vise which clamped beyond redemption even by the most frantic tugging of strong arms of a desperate man. The charger's neck was outstretched, his nostrils distended, his tail given like a banner to the breezes. As for Jones, he stuck to his saddle like a leech and whip-sawed on the reins for dear life. Despairing ideas of letting go and letting this unmanageable monster float out from under him ran through his head. But like the usual uncertain rider on a runaway he was "frozen" on.

Now they were in infantry territory. After he had gone hurtling past the first grinning group of doughboys, tugging and gasping, up within the bosom of Lieutenant Ferdinand Jones rose the pride of the artillery. With magnificent abandon, he ceased his struggle against the iron jaw of the mouse-colored momentum beneath him. He gritted his teeth and stuck out his chin against his helmet strap. Left hand grasping the reins, right resting carelessly on his pistol holster, he thundered on.

"It's the Light Brigade!" shouted somebody from a company in support, scattered by onrushing horse and rider. "The —— —— cavalry's gittin' in the war at last!"

Whining, zipping things passed, also going fast, but in the opposite direction. Perhaps Nemmy thought they were bees. Anyway, he accelerated. But Ferdy knew 'em for bullets, rifle and machine-gun bullets. An artilleryman really ought not to recognize them, but they forced an introduction on Ferdy.

As the express catapulted through the advance units, cries floated in fragments to the wind-filtered ears of the dashing lieutenant.

"Hey! What the——!"

"And Sheridan twenty miles away!"

"Turn around, you fool, you're——"

"That's Germany out there!"

"Stop him! Stop!"

Out into a stretch of open country, they went at a breakneck gallop. Nemmy was puffing hard but never slackening. Those bees were buzzing around more busily. Must be near the hive. From the parched lips of Lieutenant Ferdinand Jones, the rushing wind snatched a last prayer.

And then in mid-career, in the very center of that open space between the American and the German lines, something smote Ferdy and Nemmy with stunning force and suddenness.

It was the terrific, cataclysmic silence of 11 A.M., November 11, 1918—Armistice Day.

Nemmy faltered in his stride. His ears wig-wagged back and forth and finally set, one forward, one to the rear. Ferdy pulled him in front of a mound from which protruded the ugly snout of a machine gun.

Lieutenant Jones, Field Artillery, wheeled his mount and rode calmly back to his own lines. A German machine-gun crew, hands in the air, followed in his train.

"Just in time to see the end of the war," Lieutenant Jones grinned as he rejoined his excited battery commander. "And now, sir, I'd like to report that I have this horse thoroughly tamed. It is safe to assign him as a mount for the stable sergeant."

Indian Fighter

STEPHEN HOLT

JOE rode Baldy out to the spring on the edge of the ravine. Sliding to the ground he led the old sorrel pony over to where the clear water burbled from the ground.

"Take a last drink, pal," he whispered.

Baldy dropped his head and began to drink. Joe stared at him and thought of the time the old codger in the buckskin shirt had come along riding him. Seeing Joe standing in the barn door, he had come in and said, "Want to buy a good Indian fighter for ten dollars, Bub?"

Suddenly a coyote yipped across the ravine, jolting Joe's thoughts. And another. And another—till it seemed the air was alive with the cries. An icy wind sprang up. A snowflake hit Joe's pug nose.

"Winter!" Joe whispered, his stomach going fuzzy, and his eyes following Baldy's down the ravine to where the chemist, Mr. Graham from Omaha, prodded exploringly around in the shale. Joe's fingers twined in Baldy's mane. "And winter spells coyotes pulling you down, Baldy," he whispered. "Unless——" He broke off talking to pull a cockle burr from Baldy's mane. Joe's dad had gone broke. Graham had bought the farm. The family was clearing out for California—after his dad shot Baldy.

Baldy's head came slowly around to Joe. With old gray lips he began nibbling at a button of Joe's leather jacket.

Joe's heart turned to water. "There's no other way," he babbled. "Nobody bid you in at the sale. Mr. Graham doesn't want you. And we can't turn you loose to let them coyotes finish you in the snow."

Baldy's ears drooped. He gave a big sigh, easing his weight to his left hip, then raised his head to rest on Joe's thin shoulder.

Joe got a picture of his lonesomeness without Baldy. He began to spar with the old horse. Baldy used his head to dodge around. And the pain within Joe mounted steadily. He said, "Count three, Baldy!" using the sign they'd practiced—Joe pressing Baldy's thin old shoulder with his elbow. The kids down at the country school at the crossroads used to eat it up.

Joe felt his face go stiff with anguish at the thought of Baldy lying stiff and cold down in the coulee back of the barn where all animals were hauled after they had died.

It wasn't as though he hadn't tried to save Baldy. And his dad's farm. He had written to Graham,

Robinson and Wade, chemists at Omaha, and sent a sample of shale from the canyon, pleading, in a pencil-scrawled note, that it must be good for something.

But nothing seemed to come of it, beyond Mr. Graham coming out at the last minute—the day of the sale—to buy the farm without saying more than two words. Then he had gone wandering down along the ravine.

"Now, pretend there are Indians," Joe commanded Baldy. "Indians, Baldy. Indians!"

Dutifully, Baldy dropped to his bent old knees, then to his stomach, and finally stretched full length on the ground, his head hugging the grass. The old codger had shown Joe this.

Joe stared at the old horse stretched silently on the ground. And suddenly, something inside him stiffened. There must be a way to save Baldy. Some way. And he'd have to find it.

He clucked to Baldy to get up, then mounted him by shinnying up his side. He rode down by the barn where his dad, George Straka, stood chewing a straw and just staring around him.

His father had had a bad day. His best bay team, Rock and Babe, sold. His new plow. The two sets of brass-studded harness.

"Dad, I've just got to make a last try to save Baldy," Joe said, slipping to the ground.

George Straka looked at the sun setting in the west behind a black bank of snow clouds. "It's thirty miles to Grand Island, and your mom's anxious to get started," he said.

"If I had an hour, I could try three places," Joe pleaded. "Please, Dad, let me."

"Whose places?" George Straka's tired brown eyes probed Joe's.

"Blaha's—" Joe began.

"Got ten horses and six kids and no feed for either," George Straka said softly.

"Creswell's—"

"Plenty of money, but Thaddeus Creswell spends half his time bragging how he hasn't a horse on the place—that he's a power-machine farmer from the word 'go.' "

"I've got to try," Joe pleaded. "I just got to, Dad."

George Straka's answer was to go get a pair of shears. "I'll work on his mane," he said gently. "It'll make him look trimmer."

Joe's heart leaped. "And his hooves?" Joe asked. "He'll step better then."

His father eyed Baldy's bent old knees, his long, broken hooves, especially the right front foot with the wire scar from the time Baldy got caught in the barbed-wire fence.

"And his hooves," he agreed. "You get the hoof trimmers, Joe, while I get rid of this cockle-burred mane."

Joe got the hoof pincers and brought them to his dad. He got a bucket of water and washed Baldy's old winter coat.

In less than fifteen minutes, Baldy was a changed horse—to Joe. "Boost me on, Dad," he said.

George took Joe by the bent right leg and heaved

him on to Baldy's shining back. "One hour," he said softly. "And good luck, Joey." He looked wistfully at the boy.

Joe gently nudged Baldy's thin ribs and rode toward the gate that led to Blaha's.

"Throw in the bridle, if you make a deal," his father called.

Joe nodded, and riding out the gate, turned down the road toward Blaha's.

By the time he rode the two miles to turn in at the Blaha gate, Baldy's winter hair was plastered smooth with sweat. He looked swell. Swell! Joey gently nudged his old ribs and rode up to the ramshackle house with a flourish. Hope for a quick sale made his heart thump under his worn cotton shirt.

But suddenly, from the unpainted house, poured six Blaha kids—two sets of twin boys, a hollow-eyed girl of ten, and Jimmy, the oldest.

"Hi!" Jimmy said, eyeing Baldy enviously. "Gonna sell Baldy to Pop?"

Joe's eyes swept around toward the lean-to barn, to take in the meager pile of wheat straw—all the feed Blaha would have to pull four horses and a milk cow through the Nebraska winter. Joe shook his head and turned old Baldy to go, but Mr. Blaha came out of the barn and hailed him. Joe nudged Baldy, and with the Blahas trailing, rode down to him.

Mr. Blaha was a Pole. He had a flat face, a stub nose, and high cheek bones, but his brown eyes were warm and steady. "I hear you're going out to California," he said with a touch of envy. "Where you can pick oranges right off the trees."

Joe wished he hadn't said that. The sound of six Blaha kids sucking in their lips would be hard to shake.

"Lucky——" Jimmy muttered softly.

"I don't know," Joe said carefully. "I'd rather stick around—with Dad."

"I know—you hate to let go." Blaha's eyes swept the bleak, flat farm and came doggedly back to Joe.

But Joe caught sight of the sun, red and sinking on the western horizon. A panic seized him. Baldy's time was running out. He turned the horse's head and nudged him in the ribs.

"Well, so long," he said. "See you sometime."

Jimmy sprang to catch Baldy's bit. "Hey, wait a minute, Joe," he pleaded.

Joe pulled Baldy up, and six Blahas went into a huddle with their dad.

It wasn't hard for Joe, sitting there, to get the drift. Blaha was being crowded. His old voice trembled as he said for Joe to hear, "What can I do? I got no feed, no money!"

Joe nudged Baldy's ribs and got out of there quick.

Thaddeus Creswell was fixing a snowplow as Joe rode up to the big woven-wire gate that led to Creswell's glistening gray buildings—a huge barn, a two-story house, and a red machine shed that housed enough power machinery to start an agency.

Creswell was a big man with an open red face,

huge blue eyes, and a hearty laugh. He'd made no secret of always liking Joe. He'd even listened to Joe talk about the shale beds.

He came down to the gate and opened it to let Joe through. "Well, Joe, did you come to say good-by?" he boomed. "Wish I had sense enough to quit and go to California!" His laugh made old Baldy's ears twitch.

Joe grinned, then sobered. "I, I came to sell you Baldy," he blurted. Suddenly, the dam burst within him, and he poured out a babble of words. "Dad's got to kill him if I don't sell him in an hour," he said. "You've got a boy—buy Baldy for him. Look!"

He leaped from Baldy and pressed his elbow in his ribs. "Count five, Baldy!"

Baldy paused as if in deep thought, then pawed till Jimmy took his elbow from his ribs—five it was.

Creswell took off his Stetson. "Well, now," he said, "I'm a machine man. No horses!"

Joe's heart thumped. "Indians, Baldy, Indians!" he said sharply.

Once more, Baldy lowered his tottering frame, to the Creswell yard.

Jimmy flopped beside him and looked over his old paunch to Creswell. "An old Indian fighter," he said hopefully.

Creswell whistled softly. "What do you know—a regular circus horse!"

"Then, you will buy him—five dollars! A dollar! Fifty cents—and the bridle thrown in!" Joe's insides were one big pain. He waited—and waited.

Then a noise behind him swung him around, and there sat the reason Creswell couldn't buy Baldy—Alan, his spoiled boy, with blond, curly hair and scornful gray eyes that looked Baldy over as though he already lay dead and cold.

"Buy that old plug, Pop?" he screeched. "If you do, I'll run away from home."

Joe shinnied up the side of Baldy and got out of that yard, fast.

There remained only Mr. Graham himself as the last hope. Joe rode into their own yard and down to the spring. He circled the house and went down to the hen house. No Mr. Graham.

The gully back of the barn where all dead animals were hauled, taunted Joe. He couldn't keep it out of his eyes.

He rode over to the west fence and stared off at an evening thunderhead, as though a stack of hay might come out of it that would feed Baldy for the winter.

The gully beckoned. And still no Mr. Graham.

Joe dropped to lie along Baldy's neck, the reins lying loose. With a sigh, the old horse turned and walked toward the barn, around behind it, and down to the gully.

Joe's dad came up behind them with his thirty-thirty in the crook of his arm. He was blinking hard.

"No sale," Joe whispered.

George Straka nodded, them said gently, "You go on up to the house, Joey."

This was Baldy's finish. Joe knew it. His dad knew it. In a minute Joe'd go up the hill; when he got out of sight there'd be the sharp crack of his dad's thirty-thirty, and Baldy would drop in his tracks.

But suddenly, Joe's eyes, staring off across the fields, caught the shape of a thunderhead in the western sky. It was big and black—the shape of an old Indian warrior's head. There was a war-bonnet of fleecy lighter clouds down his back.

It gave Joe an idea.

He slipped off Baldy's back and took the rifle from his dad's hands. "You go on up the hill, Dad," he said. "I'll tend to this."

He stood and watched his dad's feet carry him over the hill. His dad knew he could shoot. Joe had killed plenty of coyotes with the thirty-thirty.

Suddenly, he came close to Baldy.

"Indians, Baldy! Indians!" he whispered.

Baldy lowered himself to the ground.

Joe flopped beside him and pulled the rifle across Baldy's neck. There would be five shots across the hill, then the sixth one into Baldy's brain. He'd lived an Indian fighter; he'd die one, too.

"One!"

A little puff of dust danced half way up the hill.

"Two!"

The whine of a bullet ricocheting from a rock came back to Joe.

Baldy lay quiet—a genuine Indian fighter, all right.

"Three! Four! Five!" whined from the gun to find distant marks.

Baldy still lay not moving a muscle. Even his eyes were closed.

Jim swung the barrel of the gun around with the muzzle pointing just back of Baldy's ear. His finger twined on the trigger—he hesitated, then closed his eyes.

"Hey!" A hand from behind knocked the gun barrel up. "What are you going to run in the milk cows with if you shoot Baldy?" Mr. Graham's voice demanded.

Joe looked around. "M-milk cows?" he stuttered. "We're moving."

Old Baldy hadn't twitched.

"Oh, no," Mr. Graham said. "You're staying—you and your dad—to run the farm. All I want is the shale beds. I've tested it and it'll make the finest unbreakable glass in the world."

Suddenly Baldy raised his head and looked Joe in the eye. "Fine thing—talking, with Indians all around," his old eyes seemed to say.

Joe couldn't help laughing.

Mr. Graham joined in.

Then Joe took Baldy's reins and clucked to him. "Come on, old timer," he said softly. "The Indians have pulled out."

"For good!" Mr. Graham nodded.

"For good!" Joe repeated, and something bubbled over in him. They started up the hill to tell his dad.

"Do you know what I'm going to do tomorrow, Mr. Graham?" he asked.

"Nope."

Joe grinned. "I'm going to buy the Blahas the biggest sack of oranges they've ever seen."

"Swell!" Mr. Graham said.

"Swell is right," Joe agreed. He gave Baldy a gentle slap along his neck and steered him into the barn.

Apple for Mom

JIM PACE

JIM and little Angus crowded close to the barbed wire fence to let the gypsy caravan pass. They stood there on the grass watching three creaking wagons filled with men, haggard women, and a raft of ragged kids file by. And then came a colt, a wonderful colt.

He was tagging the last wagon. About three years old, Jim decided, and a natural pacer with a deep satiny coat that shone in the late Alberta sun.

Angus sucked in his breath. "Like an apple," he breathed. "Shiny and round. And look at him go!" The colt, who had stopped to nip a bunch of grass, raced for the wagon.

Jim stared, and absent-mindedly jingled the two dollars and sixty-eight cents in his pocket. He was sixteen, tall for his age, and had deep-set brown eyes that were darkening with thought of tomorrow

—Mom's birthday. "Yeah," he nodded. "Some Apple for Mom's present."

An idea began to take shape within him. "Apple for Mom, with love." He could see the card in Apple's mane, and Mom's face when she came out in the morning and read it. Mom was blonde and pretty and she'd come to Alberta from Kentucky, where she'd had her own pony. She had a saddle tucked away in the house and riding clothes; and a hunger, Jim knew, which she proudly kept hidden.

Jim and Angus looked at each other, and with their tin lunch pails rattling, moved closer, down to where the men had pulled over to the side of the lane.

Apple came nuzzling up. "Gentle as a kitten," Jim whispered. "Hi, ol' boy." He rubbed Apple's left ear and listened to one of the Hungarian gypsies.

"If it snows——" The man shook his dark head.

Jim knew that snow would be serious, even fatal. Gypsy caravans often passed, but usually much earlier and headed south. This gang was on the spot.

Apple nuzzled inside Jim's leather jacket. "Hungry?" Jim said gently.

A boy on a buckskin, driving two jaded cows, came up. He stared at Jim and Angus, then rolled off his horse and moved over. "Beat it," he told them.

Jim stood his ground, feeling Angus' sturdy fist in his. "This is a Canadian Government road allowance," Jim said. "I don't have to beat it."

"Maybe you don't like us to pet Apple, here," Angus piped.

"Who?" the boy asked the dark man.

Jim grinned sheepishy. "He means the colt, here. Yours?"

"Not mine; Pop's," the boy said.

"Mister," Jim said suddenly. "Can Ang and I take the colt for a ride?"

"What's your name?"

"Jim. And this is my brother, Angus."

"My name's Slezsky," the man said, pausing from hauling out a greasy box of provisions. "Frank Slezsky. This is my boy. His name's Pete."

Jim said, "Hello!" and added, "I'll give him a feed of oats, Mr. Slezsky."

"Guess we could get him if they try any funny stuff, Pop," Pete said.

Mr. Slezsky got out an old bridle.

"Let me," Jim said, his fingers itching. He bridled Apple, wanting to laugh with glee at the way the colt nibbled the bit, then let it slide gently into his velvet mouth.

He shinnied up Apple's sleek side, then rode over to the wagon pole for Angus to hop on.

In ten ecstatic minutes they rode up in front of the house, yelling, "Mom! Mom! Look, Mom!"

Mom came out, her blonde hair shining in the setting sun. She put up a soft slim arm to Jim's, then let it slide along Apple's mane till it circled his neck. She buried her pretty oval face in his dark mane. "He's wonderful," she whispered. Jim tried to clear out. "Some gypsies are camped down here for the night," he said. "I promised a feed of oats for this plug."

"Plug!" Angus' outraged voice exclaimed.

But Mom couldn't hide the look in her eyes, and Jim found himself slipping to the ground and saying, "Mom, I'll get your saddle."

In five minutes, she was down the road, hair flying, straight in the saddle, calling back, "Like a rocking chair, Jim!"

Jim stood staring after them. Then, he turned and trudged into the house, back to the west end room that was his and Angus' bedroom. He ransacked all the bureau drawers. But the end was just what he'd known it would be: two dollars and sixty-eight cents. And a birthday card printed with a bunch of blue violets in one corner, and the mocking scarlet letters saying, "Happy Birthday."

Jim sank to a chair at his desk made from apple boxes. Solemnly, his heart leaden within him, his fingers took up a pen, and idly printed, *"To Mom, with Love. Jim and Angus."*

The soft rat-a-tat feet of Apple roused him. He stuffed the card in his pocket, along with the money, and went out.

"Oh, Jim!" Apple brought Jim's mother rocking up, his trim feet flying, head high. "He's wonderful!"

Jim's mouth tightened. His Mom's face looked really happy—not as it proudly put on when she sat down to write the judge, in Kentucky, "I've got the most wonderful husband in the world," and how they didn't "need a thing. Not a thing."

Mom got down, when Angus lugged the kitchen chair over by Apple, who didn't shy. After a moment's stare at Jim's thoughtful face, she said with a smile, "I wouldn't have time to ride anyway, dear."

It was the smile that did it.

Angus' sharp eyes were instantly wise. All the time Apple was eating his oats, in the extra stall, Angus kept hammering at Jim.

"You're crazy," he said. "Two dollars and sixty-eight cents. Why, that Hungie's sharp! He'll kill himself laughing."

Jim just walked in by Apple, his mind whirling.

"If they were going to be around, you could work it out," Angus persisted. "But you know Hungies. Like as not they'll break camp in the night."

There was nothing Jim could do but lead Apple from the stall, and with Angus on behind him, ride down to face Mr. Slezsky.

"Your dad like?" Mr. Slezsky asked.

"Mom liked—it's her birthday tomorrow," Jim said.

"Your dad——" Slezsky's eyes narrowed.

"Didn't see," Jim admitted.

Slezsky took Apple's rope. His face had suddenly grown bleak.

"Beat it," Pete said. "Pop's got enough on his mind about where we're going to hole up."

Jim and Angus slid to the ground. Jim put his hand in his pocket and brought out the money: two dollars and sixty-eight cents. "I want to buy this horse," he said earnestly.

"Two sixty-eight!" Pete exploded.

Mr. Slezsky didn't say a word.

"I could send you more," Jim explained desperately. "Just tell me where you're going——"

It was the worst thing Jim could have said. Slezsky's panicky eyes roved wildly. "Yes, where——?" he asked.

A baby's cry, cold and sickly, came from one of the wagon boxes, followed by the distracted croon of a woman trying to comfort it.

Slezsky's face twitched. "Go home," he said harshly. "And don't come back unless you got forty dollars."

"I'll be back! And I'm sorry you don't have any place to hole up." Jim took Angus' hand and lit out for home. After supper Jim wandered to the cow barn to turn out the cows for night grazing. Then, drifting toward the house, he wandered on into his bedroom. He undressed and crawled in beside Angus.

Mom came to tuck Angus in. Her hands pulled the homemade quilt around his chubby shoulders, then came over to brush lightly Jim's forehead. "Good night," she said softly. "And don't mind—about Apple! Don't mind about——"

Suddenly, she was gone. But Jim finished her sentence. "Don't mind about a birthday present,

Jim. After all, Daddy, and you boys, and this house——"

"House!" That was it! There was a house—on the Syndicate Land. A section of gumbo that an English outfit had tried to colonize and given up, leaving an old ramshackle slab house and barn by a lake. Anyone could have it—even Slezsky! Six miles up in the hills——

Jim threw on his clothes. He let himself out through his west window, and ran the half-mile to where the camp had been.

There was nothing there but a bed of burned-out coals.

He started to run down the road after them. Then he stopped. He couldn't catch them that way. But they might have turned right, to Brandin. And if he ran cater-cornered——

He caught them on the quarter-mile angle.

"Well, if it isn't 'Apple' again," Pete sneered.

"Shut up, Pete!" Slezsky said, getting down from his wagon. "You got forty dollars, kid?"

"No," Jim said. Then forgetting all about making a deal with Slezsky, and bargaining, he blurted out, "You give me Apple and I'll tell you where to hole in for the winter." He even drew a map. And with the baby wailing, and the thought of what they'd go though, Jim took the two dollars and sixty-eight cents from his pocket and thrust it, too, into Slezsky's hand.

A paper fluttered to the ground—the birthday card; but it didn't matter now.

With Slezsky's sharp eyes on his face, Jim realized the man wouldn't have to give him Apple, now. Why should he? He had all he needed to know.

"You are a good boy," Slezsky said, pocketing the money and climbing back on his wagon. "We go. Before someone else finds this place."

Jim plodded home. He was a soft dope. Mom with no birthday present, when if he'd been smart——

Then suddenly it was morning.

And Mom was bending over him. "Oh, Jim—thank you. And you, Angus." She had them in her arms. "Such a wonderful birthday present."

Jim, sleepy, didn't know what it was all about.

Outside, a horse nickered.

"Apple!" Angus leaped to the window.

They all streaked out, to let Apple snuggle his nose against Jim's blue cotton pajama top.

And the wind in Apple's mane caught the card tied to it, Jim's card: "To Mom, with love——"

Jim's eyes turned to Mom.

"A boy named Pete, on a buckskin horse, rode in," she said. "He wouldn't stay. He just said, 'Pop said to give this to that kid.' "

Mr. Slezsky would have done it last night, if he'd been sure, Jim realized.

"Boost," Angus said, and got on Apple. He rode him around in a circle—a magic circle—with Apple's trim feet flying.

"The ol' Apple!" he called in glee.

"The ol' Apple," whispered Mom, her eyes shining.

Pleasure crept up through Jim like water rising in a spring. He laughed. "The ol' Apple for Mom," he said softly. "With love."